ON THE FLY

SIERRA HOCKEY #4

ELISE FABER

ON THE FLY
BY ELISE FABER

Newsletter sign-up

ON THE FLY
Copyright © 2025 Elise Faber
Print ISBN-13: 978-1-63749-161-4
Ebook ISBN-13: 978-1-63749-160-7

SIERRA HOCKEY

CONTENT WARNING

Author's note: There are some difficult themes in this story. For CW information, please check this book's page on my website.

PROLOGUE

Joey

I'm sitting in my office and wondering how in the fuck I got here.

I mean, I know *how* I got the head coaching job for the Sierra hockey team—same as I know that part of me will never be satisfied with how it was bestowed upon me.

I didn't earn it.

Not wholly.

I'm the consolation prize, the diversity hire.

Or, at least, that's what the sports bloggers are saying.

Sighing, I settle back in my chair—what has officially become my chair over the last days—and try to get my head together.

Tonight is my official first game as the head coach of the Sierra.

I'm the first woman to ever get here.

And I need to make it count.

I need—

There's a perfunctory knock before the door opens and...

My lungs hitch.

Because the general manager of the Sierra, Damon Connors, walks in.

Tall, grumpy, sexy as hell, and built like a male model, the man is temptation personified.

I've wanted him from the first moment I laid eyes on him.

Which was approximately one second before I came to terms with the fact that I could never have him.

Not just because he's my boss—

But also because he's untouchable.

The fallen hero who clawed his way from the shadows back into the light. The avenging...not angel, because he's far from that, but the antihero with a savior complex, a soft spot for the women in his life, and a moral code that's known only to him.

He's everything I lust after.

In fact, he's so perfect for me it's like the universe peeped into my Kindle reading history and rendered a man from between the pages.

"You good?" he asks quietly, stepping close enough for me to see the scar crisscrossing his right eyebrow, the flecks of gold in his blue eyes.

I grab my tablet, loaded with everything I can possibly need to coach effectively tonight, and stand. "I'm good," I confirm as I round my desk and move toward the door—which, invariably, brings me closer to him.

His spicy male scent fills my nose.

The heat that always seems to radiate outward from his body scorches my skin.

Those intent blue eyes fix on mine...and go soft. "Joey," he says gently.

My fingers spasm, sending the tablet to the floor.

Dammit.

Quickly, I bend, trying to ignore that he's bending with me, reaching for the tablet before I can grab it. He lifts it, presses it into my hands, and I know he's reading my nerves completely wrong when he says, "You're going to be fine, Red."

Red. His nickname for me. Something that never fails to send butterflies through my middle.

And add in that gentle? To most, he's not a gentle man. But I've seen glimpses of that soft, that gentle, that nice streak...and it's my kryptonite.

Which is why I'm unable to move, staring at him even though I know I'm going to be fine out there on the bench tonight.

Sure I have nerves.

But I'm qualified and capable.

The guys like and respect me.

I've paid my dues.

I just...have the weight of female representation sitting on my shoulders *and* the hots for my boss.

No big deal.

Because as of a few days ago, I have the job I've always dreamed of.

And because of *that,* the man I've always dreamed of has become untouchable.

Something I remind myself of then and there.

I need to focus on what's ahead, not lament about what I can't have.

"I know I'll be fine."

Because I have to be.

The arena's full of fans—I can already hear the sounds of the crowd, even from our position in the bowels of the arena.

I straighten my shoulders, lift my chin, and turn to go.

But the moment I reach for the door handle, Damon is in

front of me, those blue eyes blazing. "You know I wouldn't have hired you if I didn't think you were up for it."

I don't know that.

I mean, I do.

But I don't and—

"Joey," he says, settling his hands on my shoulders, crouching a little to hold my gaze. "You're up for this."

Gentle again.

And, goddammit, my heart can't take this.

Grumpy, demanding, bordering on the edge of asshole Damon, I can deal with.

Sexy, brooding, taciturn Damon, I can handle.

But sweet, gentle Damon with the encouraging words?

Nope.

This isn't good at all.

As if it wasn't bad enough that I respect and like him, that I've wanted to explore every inch of that strong, muscled body...this whole interaction has me falling a little in love with him.

And I know he sees it.

Because he steps back as if he's been burned.

"Joey."

It's a cold rebuke.

"I need to get on the ice," I mutter, shoving by him, reaching for the handle again. My fingers close around the cool metal when his words reach my ears.

"This can't be, you know that."

I turn the knob. "I know that."

"For a hundred reasons."

Gee, thanks.

"I know that too," I say aloud, pulling the door open.

"It *can't* be."

I glance at him over my shoulder. "Damon," I say quietly.

"I'm well aware of every obstacle that stands in my way"—I hold his stare—"including you—"

He opens his mouth but I don't let him speak.

"—so just shut the fuck up and let me do my job."

Blue eyes spark with fury, kissable lips press flat, his ever-present frown deepens.

"Joey," he begins.

And I do the only sensible thing I can—

I walk away.

But when I glance back at him before I turn the corner...

The look on his face has me falling even deeper.

ONE

Joey, Eight Months Later

I ROLL my shoulders before I head for the locker room.

The team's home opener is tonight and the fans are expecting another great season.

Even with the upheaval of the previous one—our head coach getting fired because he was sexually assaulting several female staff members, including the significant other of one of the players on the team—we managed to make it to the second round of the playoffs.

Not as far as we wanted—no, the end goal is always hoisting the Cup.

But better than most people expected with the negative press, the turbulence, the change in personnel.

Because Travis Hiller wasn't the only problem in the front office.

Which is why Damon and I spent the last months working with the new owners of the team—because the previous owners sold the steaming pile of shit that was the Sierra as soon as the news broke about Hiller's toxicity—to clean house.

To keep only the players and staff who are committed to a competitive, healthy future that is built on family.

Not fucking taking what you want without care for others.

Not full of hazing and a toxic locker room.

Not dragged down by hiding bad behavior.

I hold myself to a gold standard and know so do the back and front office staff, and—more importantly—the players do.

I couldn't have done it if the guys weren't on board, if Damon wasn't equally locked into the program, along with the new owners.

But now we're starting the new season on a fresh note.

There are no hidden bad behaviors, no excuses made, no unsafe spaces that exist.

Now we just need to keep it that way.

I pause outside the doors to the locker room, hearing the guys talking inside, laughter punctuated with teasing, and know the camaraderie isn't because of me, not really.

It's Knox and Lake, Riggs and Leo, Colt and Storm. They've had my back from the moment I stepped into the head coaching job and they haven't stopped.

And because of that, the other guys fell in line.

Because of that, our new players had a stable framework to step into.

Now we're going to build on that.

Starting tonight.

I close my eyes, take a breath, push the intense off-season I spent working my ass off, the training camps and scouting trips, the time with our player development department, the practices and film I've studied, the line combinations I've tinkered with, the press conferences I've endured...I push *all* of that aside.

Tonight I get to do my favorite thing.

Be on the ice and coach some fucking hockey.

Exhaling, I roll my shoulders, open my eyes, and reach for the handle just as my assistant coaches round the corner—Tommy, Dave, and Kaitlyn. Tommy and Dave focus on defense and offense, respectively, and Kaitlyn is a new addition who sees the big picture.

She's fantastic and I cannot wait to see her grow.

But, for now, I have a team to focus on, a strategy to reinforce, a lineup to share—

"I'm ready, Coach Joey!"

Or well, a lineup to pass off to an adorable little girl who's decked out in full Sierra regalia and who is going to put the boys in their places.

Little Evie is a spitfire.

And I don't just mean her bright red hair.

She's boisterous and confident and so damned sweet I swear I'm going to get a cavity every time I talk to her.

She belongs to Ivy, the team's strength coach—one of the women who was exposed to Hiller's extremely unfortunate attention last season—and is recently adopted in all but paperwork by Knox, one of my best players.

She's also become one of the team's mascots.

Always energetic, that adorable personality, confidence for days...and thus, the perfect person to announce the roster for our first game of the season.

"Glad to hear it, peanut," I say, mouth already curving because I know exactly what she's going to say in response to that.

And she doesn't delay.

Her hands hit her hips, but she's smiling too. "I'm not a peanut."

"Oh?" I tease. "I thought all peanuts wore blue and green glitter bows."

A beleaguered sigh, her eyes rolling to the ceiling. "*Joey.*"

"No?"

She puts one hand out, palm up. "Roster please?"

"What's a roster?" I ask, doubling down. "More peanut things?"

Another sigh, but it doesn't completely hide her giggle.

And that's when I pass over the slip of paper I've written the starting lineup on.

She bounces on her toes in excitement, the twin braids her hair has been corralled into bouncing along with her. "Can I go in?" she asks.

I peek inside, make sure all pertinent parts are covered and the guys are ready for invasion by glitter-bow-wearing little girls then glance back at Evie and nod. She skips into the room without delay and I start to follow her then halt, pulse jumping, when I see Damon round the corner.

"You coming?" Evie asks, glancing back over her shoulder.

"Yeah, peanut," I tell her, nodding at my coaches to precede me. "I'll be right in." I drop my voice as Tommy passes me, murmuring, "Get started if this"—a nod toward Damon as he strides toward me, trademark scowl in place—"takes more than a couple of minutes."

"Knox!" I hear Evie cry and both Tommy and I smile.

That smile fades as he takes in Damon's expression. But to his credit—and I give Tommy a lot of credit because he's been a strong ally for me from day one—he just nods, murmurs back, "On it," then follows Kaitlyn and Dave inside.

I suck in a breath but manage to keep my expression neutral as Damon comes close—even though every nerve in my body begins to sing, to yearn. It's familiar, something I've pushed down time and again. So why would today be any different?

"What is it?" I ask after the door swings shut behind the group.

"Nothing," he mutters.

That makes my chin lift, my shoulders straighten, my frustration grow. "Is *nothing* the reason why you're down out of your tower and spreading your scowl around?"

That scowl deepens.

Something else I forgot to mention?

That over the last few months his perpetual scowl has gotten...*scowlier.*

And my perpetual barbs barbier.

As though we're both slipping toward an inevitable edge and throwing every weapon in our arsenal out to stop that fall.

Or maybe that's just me.

Maybe it's so I don't slip deeper into love with him, so I can do my job and keep my heart safe and—

"Hiller was detained at the doors," he says icily.

Every cell in my body goes still, fear and rage tangling before I manage to shove it down. "Doesn't matter," I say quietly and even I can hear my words are shaky. "H-he can't touch us now."

Can't touch *me* now.

Damon doesn't look convinced.

And I don't blame him.

Because my words don't sound all that convincing.

"Joey," he begins, face softening.

Voice gentle.

God, it's been months since I've gotten a glimpse of gentle in Damon's tone. Not since that night in my office when I revealed too much.

It threatens to melt me, to unstick those barbs and send me sliding down, down, *down*.

I can't.

I *can't*.

So, I don't.

I lift my chin again and ask, "Did security escort him out?"

Damon's face is unreadable for a long moment, but then it goes blank, that bare hint of gentle gone like so much smoke. "Yes," he says, "and I've beefed security up for after the game, along with calling the D.A."

"Right," I mutter.

Because this won't look good as his trial approaches.

"Are you—" He steps closer, voice dropping. "Are you okay?"

That Hiller was trying to get into the building?

Fuck no.

Just his name is enough to set me back eight months.

No. *Further*.

To the comments. To the unwanted touches. To the night that became—

A nightmare.

"I'm fine," I lie, tone turning deliberately chipper. "Ready for a great home opener and a kickass season. I'll catch up with you after the game—" I turn back for the locker room door.

But I don't make it so much as half a rotation.

Because Damon's hand is on my arm.

And then he's dragging me down the hall.

TWO

Damon

I SUSPECTED.

Fuck. I *suspected.*

But I didn't know.

I didn't fucking *know.*

In fact, I'd pressed her, demanded to her tell me everything, and she...

She fucking *lied.*

I turn to the right, shove into an empty conference room, and slam the door shut.

The vulnerability, the pain, the fear that had clouded her emerald eyes mere moments before all tell me that she fucking *lied.*

"Tell me, Red," I growl, stepping close, hating that when her eyes flash with anger, her chin lifts, and her shoulders straighten a bolt of desire shoots through my middle.

Sick.

I'm a sick fuck.

"We don't have time for you to have a shit fit," she snaps. "I have a game to win, and I need to focus."

She's not wrong.

I shouldn't have even told her about Hiller, not until later.

I don't even really know why my feet carried me out of my *tower*—as she'd quipped. Fucking funny, that's Joey. And beautiful. And strong. And smart. And...

A survivor.

Something that snaps me right back to razor focus.

"Tell me," I demand again.

She sighs and it's aggrieved. I don't blame her. I *can't* blame her.

This whole interaction is out of line, but I can't stop it.

The big rig's speeding downhill, its brakes not working, the runaway truck ramp shut down.

I can't stop the collision.

So...I stop trying.

"Damon," she clips. "Fuck off and let me do my—"

I move.

One second, she's an arm's length away from me.

The next, I've spun us, pinning that lush body of hers between mine and the door, putting my face in hers, holding her gaze with my own. "Stop delaying, Red, and. Just. Fucking. Tell. Me."

Wide green eyes.

Pink, pink cheeks.

The tip of a slick tongue darting out to taste plump lips.

Christ, I want to kiss her.

That, if anything, is the giant ass stop sign I need smacking me across my face.

I step back from her like I've been burned.

Unfortunately, I do it at the same time as she speaks.

And says what I knew the moment I saw her reaction

outside the locker room, what she lied about for fucking months, what she hid when it should have been exposed.

"He fucked me," she snaps.

I'm reeling from the ever more difficult job of containing the desires within me.

And. I. Jerk. Back.

Just as she says—

Fuck.

But before I can explain my reaction or come up with an excuse as to why my wanting this woman is even more of a disaster than the workplace conflict might make it seem, she lifts her chin higher, somehow staring down her nose at me even though she's a good six inches shorter.

She does all that...but I don't miss the flash of hurt in her eyes.

"And no, I didn't want him," she says. "No, it wasn't welcome. No, it wasn't my fault."

It wasn't welcome.

She didn't want it.

My rage boils up and I spin, punching my fist out. It sinks into the sheetrock, sending up a puff of dust, pain radiating through my fingers.

Too long since I've punched something.

I haven't allowed myself that luxury, that risk.

Not since—

I slam the door on that thought and spin back around to face her.

"He didn't fuck you."

Her eyes flash again, anger overtaking pain, and she opens her mouth—

"He didn't," I say. "He raped you, baby. And like you said, it wasn't your fault."

Her teeth click together, that fight leaving her—shoulders

sagging, chin sinking down onto her chest, lungs inflating on a sharp breath. "Damon," she whispers, and I hate that her emerald eyes are glimmering with tears.

"It. Wasn't. Your. Fault." I shove down my anger further, ignore the urge inside me to keep punching, keep pummeling, keep going until I beat everything around me to a bloody pulpy mess, and slowly move back to her, hating that she's trembling, hating that she flinches ever so slightly at my movements, as I draw near, as I lift my hand and cup her jaw.

There's sheetrock dust on my knuckles. And blood.

Christ.

I pull away.

"Joey—"

Her phone buzzes, and we both freeze.

Then she slips out from between me and the door.

"Baby—"

When she spins to face me, I'm shocked to see that the fight is back, that it's swelled up like a tsunami—drawn a huge distance offshore before rushing back and obliterating everything in its path. "This doesn't change anything," she hisses. "I don't need you to jump in and rescue me, superhero cape flapping behind you—"

"I'm hardly a superhero."

I'm a criminal.

I've done jail time.

Was it worth it? Yes. Would I do it again? Fuck yes. Do I give a fuck that it ended my career and fucked up my life for longer than I care to admit? No.

Because that fucker who hurt my sister doesn't live a day without the pain I left in him.

Same as the pain doesn't leave Kylie.

"I need to go," Joey murmurs.

She *does* need to go.

The team's waiting on her.

Puck drop is imminent.

But I can't just step to the side and allow her to pass.

"Joey—"

"No, Damon. Just fucking stop, okay?" She starts to shove a hand through her hair—a telltale sign that her patience has gone beyond fraying and is now at risk of snapping. "You know now. Great. That's over. *It's* over. He's going to trial, and he'll be put away. The evidence is overwhelming."

"He would go away for longer and it would be easier if you stopped hiding this shit and told somebody."

Her mouth snaps closed so quickly that her teeth click together.

Then she's moving, arm swinging, palm colliding with my cheek.

Smack!

It's louder more than it actually hurts, but I'm too stunned to react.

"How dare you?" she whispers, eyes full of tears. "How fucking dare you?" She lifts on tiptoe and leans in, her face close to mine. "Did the police believe your sister? Did the district attorney? Would a jury have sided with her when the prosecution was hard up to lean into he-said, she-said?" She drops back down onto her heels. "I shouldn't have to remind you, but they fucking didn't. Hence the reason you went full vigilante and blew up your life."

She's right.

Of course she is.

Kylie's rapist didn't even end up facing charges, and the police—and the public after I'd fucked him up—had looked at her with derision.

God, the comments on social media alone...

She was the victim of one man's fucked-up actions...and somehow it was still her fault.

Why would anything be different today? With Joey?

And why—no matter the circumstances—would Joey want to deal with that when her plate is already overflowing with misogyny and haters just because she's coaching a bunch of hockey players?

"You have no right to tell me how to deal with"—she slaps a hand against her chest—"*my* trauma."

I open my mouth to agree with her.

But she's still talking.

"*No* fucking right."

She yanks open the door.

"Now leave me alone and let me do my fucking job."

THREE

Joey

WE WON HANDILY, and the hometown crowd's voices echoed so loud through the arena that I was barely able to hear myself think.

The line chemistry was on point, our goaltending was our strong suit (something that we've struggled with in the past), and our special teams—both on the power play and the penalty kill—were outstanding.

But it was really Storm who shined tonight.

And it's him who Lake Jordan, our captain, gives this season's Player of the Game prize to.

This is something that I know speaks to the health of the locker room—namely that it's good.

A fuck-ton better than it's been over the last few years.

Better yet?

I didn't come up with the idea of a Player of the Game.

And I didn't buy the prize.

That was all the guys.

And it's funny as fuck—not to mention, full to the brim with teasing. Typical when it comes to hockey locker room shenanigans, but the bejeweled fanny pack full of snacks Lake and company came up with takes it to another level. At first glance a fanny pack doesn't seem so bad, especially one full of snacks, but because it requires the "winner" to pose with it snapped around their waist, one of the homemade cookies from a local granny who's all but adopted some of the guys on the team in hand, it's both reward and punishment.

Also typical for a hockey team.

Grandma Donna is the honorary granny who makes the cookies in the team's kitchen, but what makes this a reward and not just punishment is that she developed a special concoction just for that fanny pack.

One taste and Storm quit bitching about the pictures.

Partly because her concoction is delicious (I got my own batch of the chocolate peanut butter balls) and partly because the normally trustworthy Riggs said the photo was for Donna herself, to let her know her gift was appreciated.

Of course, if that photo happened to make its way to the social media team and *happened* to find its way online...well, it's nobody's fault, really.

And considering I've already seen the picture pop up on the team's socials, I know the normally strait-laced Riggs has been influenced by his mischief-making wife, Ella—the sister of his teammate and mischief-maker extraordinaire, Knox.

I love that for Riggs.

The newfound twinkle in his eyes. The fact that he's not just sitting and brooding in the corner.

He's *more*.

And, coach or not, I care about the guys.

So, I love the shenanigans and I love how happy Riggs is

with Ella, how happy Lake is with Nova, how happy Knox is with Ivy.

I know it's because they've found women who fulfill them, who match them in respect and devotion and love, and even though that's not destined to be my future, I'm glad for the guys to have that.

Plus, it makes for great social media.

Winking at Lake, I clap him lightly on the shoulder. "Nice."

And then I leave the guys to it.

I have press to talk to and my players just want to chill out, fuck around, and cut loose after a successful game. They don't want the person who decides their playing time to hang about and cramp their style.

But I still feel a pang of jealousy, of missing the camaraderie so much it hurts to breathe—it's been a long time since my college hockey days were ended by an injury that meant I transitioned from playing to coaching, but I don't think the yearning to be part of a team in that way is something that ever goes away.

Not for me, anyway.

I ignore the pain, the tightness in my lungs, and I deal with the press, give my interview, make my soundbites. Before I can end it and head for my office so I can finish with my post-game tasks, a question carelessly tossed across the room sends my blood boiling.

"How do you think that spending so much time rebuilding the Sierra has impacted your love life?"

What the *actual* fuck?

The room goes quiet and still, and swear to fuck, if I heard a romcom record scratch, I wouldn't be surprised.

And I certainly don't miss the wide-eyed glances the other reporters exchange.

My temper spikes. I just want to enjoy the win, ignore the shit that Damon churned up. I just want to do my fucking job without assholes jabbing at me, trying to get a reaction that will undermine my position.

But...misogyny.

Which isn't entirely fair. Or maybe it's not completely true.

Yeah, there are still assholes out there on social media, critiquing every move I make. But they're quieting, coming fewer and further between.

It's just...exhausting.

Having to be perfect and always composed and constantly walking a tightrope—being feminine and approachable and *don't forget to smile* battling with just wanting to have the freedom to do my job like my male counterparts are able to.

But that's not my reality.

I'm the first female coach in the league, and the expecta-tions—*my* expectations—are high.

I open my mouth, staring at the young twenty-something male who looks vaguely familiar. He's wearing a smug expres-sion on his face, and I feel a sharp retort zip toward the tip of my tongue. Then I glance around the room, some of my rage tempered by the looks on the rest of the reporters' and sports bloggers' faces.

Shock. Annoyance. *Outrage.*

And not just from the women.

A breath centers me. This too shall pass.

Another has my reply coming to mind.

This isn't the first time some asshole wants me to lose my cool and mouth off, and while some of the coaches in the league can get away with their fiery responses and well-known tempers, I don't have that same luxury.

For the moment, that's reality.

I have to be calm and collected, lest I'm emotional.

I have to be measured and successful, lest I'm impulsive.

I have to be *perfect*, lest I don't belong here.

Not with everyone.

But still with enough people that I'm always—fucking *always*—aware of the double standard of being a female coach in this league.

So, I don't mouth off.

Instead, I look at that group of men and women who are annoyed by the question on my behalf, and ask, "Anyone have any real questions?"

"I—" the smug fuck, who definitely looks vaguely familiar, though I can't place from wear, begins to protest.

"I noticed you transitioned to an offensive-focused defense for tonight's game," one of the men asks over the protesting child. "Is that a plan you intend to stick with?"

"When we have players like Riggs Ashford protecting our blue line, it would be stupid to not utilize his skills. And what he brings to our defense as a whole..."

Thankfully, my answer draws everyone back on track and by the time I call it and head for my office, I haven't been asked any other absurd questions. Of course, I don't make it free and clear. I'm stopped by some of my other coaches in the halls— Ivy checks in with me about a strength session later in the week, my head video coach lets me know my tape is ready, and Kaitlyn tells me that the practice plan for our ice in two days' time is in our shared drive.

Everything's working as it should.

Which means that I get through my post-game tasks with ease and it's not terribly late when I head to the parking lot and get in my car.

The night is clear, the stars overhead sparkling, and there's that cool kiss of fall sinking into winter hanging in the air.

We'll have snow soon and then Christmas will be around the corner and that's my favorite part of the year.

I can't wait.

Which is why I'm smiling when I pull into my driveway.

Unfortunately, that smile fades.

Because the moment I reach for the button to open the garage door, I realize—

I'm not alone.

FOUR

Damon

I KNOW that I've fucked up the moment panic tears through Joey's face.

"Fucking dumbass," I mutter, quickly stepping out of the shadows.

Mere hours before, I told her that Hiller was escorted out of the arena.

And Hiller knows where she lives.

And I'm standing in the darkness of her fucking porch, waiting for her to come home.

Dumb as shit.

I stop at the top of the few steps, standing in the bright spot of light, making sure she sees it's me.

And I know the moment that processes because her face goes carefully blank and then she reaches up to the visor again.

The garage door rumbles open, and she pulls in.

Then it rumbles shut behind her.

I turn around and wait by the front door as lights turn on

inside, as the faint sounds of her moving around on the other side of the wood reach my ears.

Then I wait some more.

I wait so fucking long I consider that she may not actually open the door to me.

Not that I blame her.

Still, I don't leave, just lean back against the pillar, keep my eyes on the door, know that the camera doorbell has likely picked up my movement. If she looks at the feed, she'll see I'm in for the long haul.

And five minutes later, the cold biting at the exposed skin on my hands and face and throat, I know she realizes that too.

Because the light just beyond the door turns on, shining through the long window on one side of it.

I hear a *click* and then the handle turns, the door swinging back enough for her to stand in the opening. Her brows flick up in silent question, but she doesn't otherwise move. She sure as shit doesn't step back, push the door wide, and invite me in like all the other times I've come over before.

"No beer?" I ask dryly.

The frost in her expression grows, ices over.

Yeah, not my finest moment, but sometimes the smart ass just doesn't want to stay buried.

"What are you doing here, Damon?" she asks.

"You going to let me in?"

"It's late." The door closes an inch. "We can talk tomorrow." *Or never.* Though she doesn't speak the last two words aloud. I just read them in her furious expression. But when she goes to shut the door, I react without really thinking, catching the panel before it latches, slowly pushing it inward.

She fights me for a second, but I'm stronger and, though she's stubborn as shit, she's not as stubborn as I am in this moment.

I don't want to move fast and risk the door hitting her.

But I'm going to win this battle. So, I keep pushing, gaining inch by slow inch until the door is open wide enough for me to push inside.

"Why are you—"

I close the door behind me, throw the lock, and lean back against it.

She clamps her mouth closed, a muscle flickering in her cheek, but she doesn't argue further, just spins on her heel and takes off for the kitchen.

I follow uninvited, figuring that I'm in for a penny at this point so I may as well be in for a pound, and reach the kitchen just as she slams the door to the fridge closed and turns with a beer in hand. With *one* beer in her hand.

Right, I guess that answers my earlier question.

No beer for me.

She moves to the counter, yanks open a drawer, and pulls out a bottle opener.

Pop!

The cap hits the trash and then she wraps her fingers around the neck of the bottle, lifts the beer to her lips, and drinks deeply.

I ignore the pulse in my dick at the sight of those plump lips wrapped around the top of the bottle, ignore that I want it wrapped around other things, and move to her, not stopping until the toes of my shoes are against the toes of hers.

Her eyes are wide, but the ice doesn't melt.

"I'm sorry," I murmur.

A crack in that exterior, surprise flickering through the emerald depths. But she doesn't reply, just sips from the bottle.

"I was out of line," I go on. "I shouldn't have pressed you, not before the game."

"Just another time," she mutters, eyes sparking with frustration as she tips back the bottle again.

I lean forward, snag the bottle from her.

"Hey!" she snaps.

I ignore her and down the last of it, the cool bite of the brew hitting the perfect spot. I look at the label, note the local brewery, and file that bite of knowledge away. Then I set the bottle aside, taking advantage of that movement to cage her in between my body and the counter.

Soft, lean curves brush against my front, setting it alight, reminding me of why I always keep my distance.

She's too fucking tempting.

She's not fucking for me.

I can't risk it. Can't risk *her*.

But right now, close like this, every cell in my body screaming at me...that's a lot harder to remember.

That fucker hurt her, *raped* her, and she's borne that silent hurt for too long.

"Yeah, Red, it would have been another time," I say, crouching a little to hold her gaze. "I would have discovered the truth eventually. I've known something was eating at you for a while, and I thought it was the job. If I knew that Hiller—"

Rage crawls up the back of my throat, wrapping tight fingers around my neck, making it almost impossible for me to force my next words out.

But they *do* come out.

In a rasping rage.

"If I knew that asshole touched you too, I would have fucking *killed* him." She jumps, green eyes flaring. "He would have disappeared between one day and the next and no one would ever have found his body—except, maybe, for the big ass black bears that I'd feed his body parts to."

Wide eyes go even wider.

But then her expression locks down. "You wouldn't, Damon," she whispers. "You fucking *couldn't*."

That's where she's wrong.

The anger in me, the constant thrum just beneath the surface, always held carefully in check, but always threatening to escape my grasp—it would love to escape, love to be set free on Hiller.

No.

I can't risk it.

"I could have." My fingers brush over her cheek. "I *would* have."

She shakes her head, as though she doesn't see how dangerous I am.

"Joey—"

"Damon," she says on a sigh, "I don't know why you're pushing this. Me telling you before tonight would have changed nothing. I wouldn't have gone public, Hiller was already fucked, and the most important thing in your life is the team. The shit that I went through would have jeopardized that further."

I still.

Does she honestly think in her fucked-up world that the shit that man did to her is less important than my dedication to my fucking *job?*

My answer to that mental question comes with her next words.

Because she *does* believe that.

"I have no evidence. I have nothing but my word against his, and after that night..." Her voices breaks. "He left me alone. It was like he did that shit and then it was over and done. So, there was no point. I went to therapy and it took a long time, but I found my enjoyment in sex again. But—" Her eyes close, a single tear sliding down her cheek. "I didn't know about Ivy and the others...I should have, and if there's any argument about me speaking up, it's that. If I had done that, they would have been safe. But I didn't and everything went down and... then it didn't matter at any longer. The most important was refocusing on the team, getting it cleaned up, and moving everyone forward."

"It wasn't more important than you, Red."

Her body jerks, as though those words surprise her.

Jesus Fucking Christ.

"The team was our focus. That's how it had to be." The words come fast and furious, as though she's desperate to convince me...and herself. "It's what the guys and staff needed. It's what Ivy and the others needed. It's what you—"

"Don't," I rasp.

Another sharp shake of her head. "It's what you needed, and I needed to give you that."

Fuck.

I don't think about all the things that are wrong in this scenario, about all the fucked-up shit inside me. Not right then.

I just...react.

I wrap my arms around her and draw her flush against me.

"I didn't need you to do that." My words are like gravel, even as I can begin to understand her fucked-up logic, can appreciate that she was trying to protect me. I *understand.* But I'm mad as hell and I want to shake her until she sees how wrong that was.

But...I need to hold her more.

So, I just draw her nearer, wrap my arms more tightly around her, and I listen as she gives me more of her fucked-up logic.

"You've already been through so much with your sister and I didn't want you to have to revisit it and"—a shrug of her slender shoulders—"you didn't even like me anyway, so it wouldn't bother you."

See?

Fucked up.

So much that the lid I keep slapped tight on all things Joey pops off and the truth I've wrestled with for so long slips out.

"I like you far too much, baby."

She goes statue still.

And then she bursts into tears.

FIVE

Joey

THIS IS PRETTY MUCH my worst nightmare—

Except, it's not.

I've already lived through that.

But it's a close second—crying in front of Damon—after being vulnerable with him not once but twice today.

I can't.

I fucking *can't.*

But the tears have built and they explode out of me without warning, without me having any hope of holding them back.

His arms were already around me, but now they move again, shifting and scooping me up. And then I'm being lifted, being held against his chest, being carried into the other room. I suck in breaths as he walks, trying to get control of myself, hating that I'm totally spiraling, loud, hiccupping sobs shaking my body.

He sinks down onto the couch with me still in his arms and I know I should pull away.

But I can't get my breath back, can't stop the tears from flowing, the sobs from hitching through my lungs.

It's like now that the truth is exposed to this man, I can't stop the memories of that night, from the weeks and months after, the guilt in discovering I wasn't the only victim...they're all flowing forward and swallowing me whole. It doesn't matter that I've hashed this out in a therapist's office, presumably made peace with my decision.

The bandage covering that deep, oozing wound inside me has been torn free and I'm just bleeding and *bleeding*.

Damon holds me closer, one hand lightly brushing up and down my side. "Let it out, baby," he murmurs, "just let it out."

"I-I-I—" A great heaving breath, tears still streaming down my face. "I c-can't," I rasp. "If I let it out, I'll n-never be able to sh-shove it d-down and l-lock it away a-again."

"Okay, Red," he murmurs, that hand running gently along my side. "Okay, baby. That's okay. Just take your time and breathe. Just breathe," he repeats, still gentle, saying it over and over again until somehow I *can* breathe, the sobs aren't hitching quite so fiercely through my lungs, the tears are slowing, no longer cascading down my cheeks.

Then the crying jag is done and embarrassment is creeping in.

No.

It's *raging* in.

As though sensing that shame building in me—or more likely, feeling my body growing stiffer, he shifts me, turning me so I'm straddling his lap.

I gasp, shock and horror warring...and then desire winning out.

How many times have I dreamed about him holding me close, about me sitting on him like this—only doing it naked while I ride his hard cock and bring us both no little amount of pressure.

Though, my fantasies always end with him over me, staring deeply into my eyes as he pounds into me.

And how fucked up am I?

Thinking about his dick after telling him about Hiller.

I'm shattered, broken, tainted—

No.

That's not me.

Something bad was done to me, but that doesn't mean I've stopped living—

Doesn't it?

The cold, calculating voice inside me is sharp and angry, jabbing deep, choosing the most sensitive, vulnerable spots.

Because I worry that it might be true.

I have my dream job. I have the team. I have a house and a car and food in the fridge. So, yeah, I have a life, and even if it's not completely living up to the fantasy that I had as a kid, as a teenager, even as a rose-colored-glasses wearing college graduate, even if I'm not living exactly how I expected all those years ago, I'm old enough to know that reality isn't fantasy.

Old enough to know that I'm far luckier than so many people in my world.

"What are you thinking?" he murmurs, running the backs of his knuckles along my cheek.

Maybe it's because it's late.

Maybe the tears ripped the shield away from my body and I have no hope of hiding myself from this man, not any longer.

Maybe it's the quiet way he asked or that kryptonite of gentle in his eyes.

Maybe it's just that I'm tired and can't continue to fight, can't keep this all inside any longer.

No matter the reason, I don't keep my thoughts to myself.

"That I'm lucky," I whisper.

His eyes flare, anger edging into the blue-gold depths.

I keep talking before his temper can take over.

"And I was thinking that while I'm not living the life I thought I would and it's not perfect, I have good beer in the fridge and food in my cabinets and a car with a full gas tank."

"Baby," he murmurs.

Gentle.

Kryptonite.

Dammit.

He runs his fingers along my jaw, dips roughened fingertips into my hair.

Undone, I keep talking, the words flowing faster, the truth slipping free. "And despite all of that, I feel like I'm constantly bleeding out. Like no matter how much gauze I pack into the wound in my belly, it's still oozing. This job is all I ever wanted and yet it's brought me more nightmares than I ever expected, and I don't know how to live with that. I don't know how to live with the fact that I finally have it all and somehow...it's all empty."

That sounds stupid.

Insane.

Fucked up.

But I can't take the words back.

And I can't help but feel—

"You're empty, baby?"

Even him saying that makes me want to cringe, to feel guilty and ungrateful.

To hide from the truth.

"I should be fine," I say. "I'll keep going to therapy and get over it and thank the lucky stars that I'm still alive to live this dream of mine."

Should. *Should.*

Fingers sliding deeper into my hair, tilting my head back, forcing me to hold deep blue eyes.

I'm lost for a moment in the beauty of them—indigo and navy woven together with golden specks—and my guard slips further.

Hell, it's long gone now.

So when he asks again, "You're empty, baby?" I can't hold back.

I just nod.

"Well," he murmurs, hand shifting, drawing me against his chest, keeping me so close that his next words are hard to hear over the sound of his steady heartbeat. "Then we'll see about fixing that."

SIX

Damon

IT TAKES a long time for her to fall asleep.

But the time for words and tears has passed, and I just hold her against me until her body relaxes against mine, until she slumps in my lap.

And then I lift her carefully in my arms, carry her up to her bedroom, and tuck her under the covers.

When she shifts uneasily, I brush my fingers lightly through her hair.

And when she settles again, I tuck the blankets tighter around her.

And *then* I leave, locking the door behind me, and driving away from her house, speeding through dark roads, mind filled with fury and need and...

Fury.

It stays inside me until I got home, until I park in my garage, until I push through the door.

Then it threatens to burst.

Thankfully, it only takes a few more steps to make it to my home gym.

And a few more after that to get to the punching bag.

Which brings me to now, my knuckles bruised and bleeding, the bag dented and swinging so hard it threatens to come down from the ceiling altogether.

And the rage inside me hasn't abated in the least.

I want to drive straight to Hiller's place, yank the asshole out of bed, and commit murder.

But I've made that mistake before—and although I stopped short of actually committing murder, it still imploded my life... and more importantly my sister's.

Who—

I catch a flash of dark brown in the mirror then jerk, spinning to see Kylie leaning back against the open doorway, her hair sleep-mussed, but her eyes far too alert for the middle of the night.

"I could hear you all the way upstairs," she says quietly.

Fuck.

I spin back toward the bag, wanting to start punching all over again, this time with the addition of my guilt and frustration for not being able to protect my sister from all manner of things big and small, even tonight from interrupted sleep.

I don't want to stop punching.

The rage inside me is still there, swirling and red-hot.

But I bypass the bag and go straight for the stack of towels, grabbing a couple and using one to mop my forehead and the other to wipe the blood from my knuckles.

When I turn back, she's gone, but I know it's not because she's returned to bed.

And my proof of that is when she returns, two bottles of beer in hand.

She passes one over to me and says, "Leave the suit by your hamper and I'll take it to the dry cleaners tomorrow."

I glance down at myself, see my jacket and shirt are wrinkled, sweaty, and spotted with blood.

Probably too far gone for even the dry cleaner to salvage, but I'm not one to deny my sister anything.

"Okay, Ky." A beat. "Thanks."

She tilts her head down the hall and I start following her, stopping to flick off the lights in the kitchen as we go.

It's not until we're climbing the stairs to our bedrooms that she bumps her shoulder against mine. "Wanna tell me what brought you trying to break another punching bag on?"

I don't.

I really fucking *don't*.

But all I say is, "I found out more shit about Hiller."

She sucks in a breath, and I hate the shadow that crosses her face.

We reach the top of the stairs, and when she's safe enough away to not fall right back down them, I bump my shoulder lightly back against hers. "It's not my story to share, kid," I explain softly. "But it's not good."

She looks up at me, blue eyes studying mine closely. "It's not *not good*," she says quietly. "It's *bad*."

I exhale quietly.

Then agree, "It's bad."

Her eyes fill with tears, but she doesn't let them escape. She hasn't cried—at least not in front of me—not since I first found out what the man did to her. And tonight is no different. She blinks a couple of times, takes a few deep breaths, and then she nods, expression growing determined.

"So, how are you going to make it better for her?"

Like that's a given.

Like it's a given that I have the power to make everything better.

It's all empty.

Joey's words slide through my mind, sad and soft and punctuated with tears. And behind all of that, a steel framework I've always been in awe of. To the world she's a woman who's breaking barriers, who is leading a male-dominated organization without fear. But I always knew she was more—yes, she has a spine of steel, yes, she has no problem calling me or any of the guys on our shit. Yes, she's a good leader and smart and hardworking and funny as fuck—

But she's so much more than that.

And the biggest part of the *more?*

It's the temptation to take something I shouldn't.

That I *can't.*

More so now that I know about Hiller.

Yet, looking into my sister's knowing gaze, critically aware of the gnawing ache inside of me that's been getting harder and harder to ignore as the years and months drift by, Joey's confession still ringing through my mind, and I know that my sister isn't wrong.

Joey is empty.

Alone.

She's been hurt.

There's absolutely no way, knowing all of that, seeing the impact it's having on her, knowing the shit my sister lived through after what was done to *her,* and knowing the woman Joey is beyond all she's survived and *not* do something about it.

It's a done deal.

Something I know my sister knows too because her expression gentles, the glossy sheen of those tears comes back, and she reaches up to pat my cheek.

"You're a good man, big bro."

"I'm—"

Before I can finish the protest—that I'm pretty much as far from a good man as they come—she drops her arm and disappears into her bedroom, beer in hand.

I have no choice but to go into my own room—because it's either that or stand there, staring at her closed door, far too many troubling thoughts ricocheting through my head. But even as I finish off my beer, dump my filthy suit on the floor next to my hamper, and drop into bed, those thoughts don't go away.

And I don't know what's worse.

Knowing what happened to Joey.

Or knowing that I'm going to be the one to fix it.

SEVEN

Joey

I'M SITTING on my back porch with a glass of wine, my tablet open, my notebook beside it, my laptop beside *that*.

Pens and pencils are strewn on the old wooden table's surface.

The threat of a splinter is always imminent when I work out here, but the weather is changing and I know soon enough that I'll need a blanket...and then a parka...and then, when winter really hits, I'll be stuck inside, staring longingly out at my back yard.

Today, it's chilly.

But today, I have the fresh air and the soft trill of birds in the trees, and the wind gently bouncing the pine needles on the evergreens in my yard.

Practice plans have been reviewed and tweaked, drills added as needed, line combinations written up and stored away—Lake is our strongest forward by far, but his wife, Nova, had her baby not too long ago and though I don't doubt his commitment to the team, I know that he's not sleeping much and milestones come quick and babies and moms get sick.

I want to provide flexibility, not just for him, but also for the rest of my guys.

Yes, they're multi-million dollar athletes.

But they're not robots.

They're people with families who need understanding and compassion—at least on the team that I want to build.

So, I'm making that happen.

Along with reviewing tape from last night's game—and not just ours. Coast to coast, there were eight games and we'll be facing off with most of those teams in the coming months.

I need to know what systems they're running, how their chemistry is looking, and what player and/or roster changes we need to make to match against of all those things. We've been honing stuff on our side throughout the off-season, but that's the micro we can control versus the macro of the other teams in the league.

So, I need to be aware of what's happening with other teams too.

And I need to know how the guys on our AHL team are looking too. Who's ready to be brought up for a game or two to keep growing their skills, who we need to find a spot on the roster because they're ready for The Show, and who needs more games to develop, or—always the hardest part—who we need to move in order to better the team as a whole.

It could be they don't fit in with our system, with the culture we're building.

Or, worse, it could be that they do but we need to trade for a different type of player anyway.

I'm not alone in my quest to digest all of this information.

I have a video team and a player development department.

I have assistant coaches and... My lungs freeze. Because I also have...

Damon.

I close my eyes, clenching my teeth together, ignoring the sharp bolt of pain that shoots along my jaw.

There's a reason I'm out here with my notebook and pens, my tablet and my laptop, and it's not just because I like to work —though, spoiler alert, I do. But it's also because I'm trying to avoid what happened last night...same as I'm trying to avoid the fact that I woke up with sun streaming in through my bedroom window.

And that I did it alone.

Because Damon had carried me there.

He'd torn the truth out of me and...

He left.

I reach for my glass of wine, take a big sip, and I do it hoping that it'll dull the sharp edges of last night.

Of course, he left.

What was he going to do? Crawl into bed next to me?

Maybe only in the pages of the romance novel currently taking up space on my Kindle.

The reality is that he's my boss.

And now he knows shit I can't take back, knows some of the raw and wounded parts of me.

And after finding out...he left.

Which is as clear a message as I've ever received.

He's still my boss—*only* my boss.

The only thing that's changed is that he now has the knowledge to more effectively manage my skills.

And that's it.

There. *Done.*

I take another gulp of pinot grigio, beg it to do its job and start numbing the edges of my thoughts.

Unfortunately, I'm about three more glasses away from that being my reality.

So, it's down to refilling my glass and hoping that fresh air and work tire me out enough so that I can sleep tonight.

If that doesn't work...maybe I'll take up hiking.

I snort as I lean forward to replay a clip one of the video coaches pulled, but my finger doesn't make contact with the screen because—

"What's funny?"

I scream.

There's no hiding it. The sound that comes out of me is nothing short of ear piercing, and even as I'm scrambling toward my sturdiest pen—the better to do a stabby-stab with—my panic is fading, my subconscious already recognizing the person the voice belongs to.

The *man* the voice belongs to.

I glare over at Damon, barely resisting the urge to clamp a hand to my chest, the better to steady my racing heart. "You're adding breaking and entering to your stalking and kidnapping charges?" I ask drolly.

His lips twitch, but he doesn't move except to cross his ankles and lean back more heavily against my deck railing.

"Hanging on your porch till you come home and taking you somewhere private for a conversation don't exactly count as stalking and kidnapping." He lifts a shoulder in an indolent shrug. "And it's not breaking or entering if you leave the side gate unlocked."

I scowl. "Not sure that argument would hold up in court."

"Good thing we're not in court then."

Ugh. Why is this man so infuriating?

"You going to tell me why you're here?" I grumble.

Another lazy shrug.

"You going to leave?"

One more lackadaisical lift and fall of his shoulders that has me seeing red.

I clench my teeth together then ask archly, "How about we move on to harassment? Or trespassing?" I flick up my brows. "Seems as though you're a repeat offender on both those counts."

His lips twitch.

"Do either of those ring a bell?" I press.

"Never heard of them," he says, his tone dry, and because he pairs it with pushing off the railing, his big body looking all sorts of gorgeous in a pair of jeans and tight black tee, I'm momentarily struck silent, any hope of a retort stuck in my throat.

Especially as he comes close, his gaze running over my set up, his eyes dragging along the papers and the document on my laptop screen, the paused video on my tablet.

Then he turns to me, those deep blue eyes searching mine.

"Did you even take a break today, Red?"

The endearment is a visceral stab to my heart and I can't guard against it, can't keep my reply in. "I got wine," I blurt.

His stare flicks to my mostly empty glass then comes back to mine.

"Does that mean you didn't eat either?"

I open my mouth, this time ready to make some excuse.

But my stomach beats me to the punch.

Because it rumbles loud enough to wake the dead.

EIGHT

Damon

HER LITTLE SHRIEK of surprise was cute.

Her listing off the various "crimes" I've committed was funny as fuck.

Her befuddlement at me asking if she ate was adorable.

But the way her cheeks go bright pink and her hands clamp over her belly when her stomach rumbles may be the sweetest thing I've ever seen.

Except for the fact that she's clearly hungry.

I push down the anger...along with the urge to wind my hand into her hair, tilt her head back, and kiss her until other things turn pink. In fact, the urge to taste her is so intense that the only thing that stops me from taking what I so desperately want is...everything she told me last night.

I'm trying to fix this shit for her, not add to her trauma.

So, instead of doing what I want, I grasp the top rung of her chair, drag it back from the wooden table that looks like it should have been put out of its misery a decade ago. I reach forward, snag her mostly empty glass of wine, shove it into her hand, and then stack all the shit she has out here into one pile.

"What the hell are you—?"

I lift the pile, thinking it's a fucking miracle I manage to corral all the pens and pencils, then turn for the house. "Come on," I tell her as I push inside.

"Damon—"

But I let the door swing shut behind me, cutting off her protest.

I stride through the hall, turning right, moving into her office. The desk and shelves are pristine...something I know is always the case because this woman never wants to work behind a desk. She's always on her back deck or in the arena, papers strewn around her, the pens and notebooks and laptop and tablet in easy reach.

Gotta be hell for her ergonomics.

I dump the papers, pens, and other shit on the empty desk, plug her laptop into the charger, and turn around.

She's standing in the open doorway, fury pulling the lines of her face into sharp relief.

Her mouth opens again.

I move close, snag the now empty wineglass, and gently flick up beneath her chin. "Yell at me in five minutes, Red," I order lightly, on the go again, this time turning in the direction of the kitchen and opening her fridge.

It takes thirty seconds of those five minutes to pull out the bottle of wine, to top off her glass. Then another thirty to return it to her hand.

"I'll be right back."

Another drop of that mouth. This time it snaps shut after a heartbeat, the click of her teeth loud enough that I bite back a wince.

"Easy, Red."

Her eyes narrow, but I just grin and tug at a loose strand of her hair, the same one that always escapes from her ponytail to lay across her eyes.

"Stop it," she mutters.

I take advantage of her batting my hand away, of her scraping her fingers through that wayward strand, battling with getting it tucked behind her ear, and zip back into the hall, walking to the front door, and tugging it open.

I bend and grab the bags I stowed there when she didn't answer the door and I knew I'd have to track her down on the back deck, straighten, then shift back inside, closing the door and locking up behind me.

"What the hell are you doing, Damon?" she snaps as I turn around.

Her hands are on her hips, one toe tapping impatiently.

Fuck, she's adorable.

And she's asking a question for the ages, one I already knew the answer to and yet wrestled with far too late last night.

An answer which inevitably means...I'm here now.

"You haven't eaten," I say instead of providing her with an actual answer. "And I brought you something you'll love."

Her eyes flick down to the bags in my hand then back up to my face and my dick twitches when she licks her lips, desire sliding through her expression. "You brought Dragon Delight?"

I start for the kitchen again. "It's your favorite," I say by way of explanation.

"But—"

I drop the bags on the counter, start pulling out containers, naming their contents one by one. "Wonton soup with extra wontons. Pork fried rice. General Tso's chicken. Lo mein with extra bean sprouts and crispy tofu. And for dessert"—I open the other bag, grab out the box that's not from Dragon Delight, but from the bakery down the street, Sweet Treats—"Peanut butter sundae pie."

Her mouth opens.

Closes.

Then opens again.

"I don't understand," she whispers, her eyebrows dragging together.

"You're hungry," I tell her, tugging on that loose strand of hair again before turning for the freezer and safely stowing the dessert where it won't melt before we can devour it. "I'm feeding you."

Confusion in gorgeous green eyes. "But you didn't know I was hungry."

"Hungry or not, are you ever going to turn down food from Dragon Delight and Sweet Treats' peanut butter sundae pie?"

For the first time since I showed on her porch, humor slides into her eyes.

But when she opens her mouth, I know she's going to lie.

"Truth," I press.

Her mouth ticks up even though she gives a beleaguered sigh and begrudgingly agrees, "Truth." Then she sighs again and this time it's quiet, her eyes sliding away from mine, discomfort bleeding into her expression.

"Good girl," I say, because when she's mad at me she forgets to be embarrassed.

And maybe also because I want to see her reaction, because when she's full of fire and steel instead of sadness and shadows, I feel like I'm not totally fucking up this up with her, that I might seriously have a chance at fixing it, of filling that emptiness inside her.

And also because when she's spitting fire, her eyes sparking, the color high on her cheeks...

I want to kiss her.

Maybe that makes me a glutton for punishment.

But I don't care.

"Just when I'm starting to think you're not an asshole, it comes right back out again."

I snort, tug at her ponytail this time, and turn for the cabinet I know houses her plates. I've been here often enough for planning sessions that I know where everything is, and maybe I've also...dreamed about fucking her on nearly every surface. "You'll think differently when you have some wonton soup and lo mein filling up your mouth."

There's a blip of quiet.

I turn back.

She lifts her eyebrows, the blip of humor sparking across her face again. "You wanna rephrase that, boss man?"

I lift mine right back. "You want me to?" And fuck it all, I don't know why I say what I say next.

There's no excuse for it.

But it just...fucking slips out.

"Or do you want me to fill your mouth up with something else?"

NINE

Joey

MY MOUTH DROPS OPEN.

Because...

Had he just said that?

Seriously. Had he just said *that*?

My mind is spinning so quickly I can barely keep my feet—one second I'm shriveling up from embarrassment, another I'm pissed that he's being pushy as fuck and stepping over every boundary we've erected in our relationship. The next I'm confused because are we boss and employee or are we—what I thought we were—co-workers who are friendly (even if I lust after him)? Or are we something completely different—as in a man and a woman who are dancing around each other because we have mutual attraction?

The last one doesn't make sense.

Because Damon doesn't do messy.

Doesn't do connection.

Doesn't do women.

Or, at least, he doesn't do anything more than scratching an itch and then moving right the fuck on.

How do I know this?

I've seen the women making their way up to his hotel room on road trips...and then making their way right back down a couple of hours later.

Same as I've seen the women meet him at the arena...and then be dropped back off at their cars to drive themselves home.

Is it pathetic how much I know about this man's habits? Yes.

Did I work late in the bar or late at the arena to feed that sick pit inside me that was desperate for any and all knowledge of this man? Also...*yes.*

And does any of that knowledge I've gained over the last years—but especially over the last months—help me make sense of what the fuck is going on here?

Nope. Absolutely fucking *not.*

We've eaten together enough that he knows my favorite places, my favorite foods *from* those places, but this isn't about work.

I don't know what it's about. A lie, but one I'm clinging to because—

We'll see about fixing that.

His voice from last night rolls through me, and even though it was soft and gentle, it struck even deeper than the innuendo that's cast me mute in this moment.

Which is why I clamp my mouth shut, brush by him to yank open the cabinet door, and reach in to grab some plates and bowls.

He's here.

He's male, which means he's stubborn.

I need to ride this out before he'll leave—and I *know* he'll leave.

The plus is that I get my favorite food while I'm stuck on this ride I never wanted to get on in the first place—

Liar.

I close my eyes for a heartbeat, shove that thought down, tucking it right next to the pulsing, throbbing need I've buried for too long. It's covered with heavy sheets of steel—the reminders that this can't be, that he's not capable of giving me what I need, what I want...even if it *could* be.

And the heaviest sheet of all is that a man like Damon would never, fucking *never* want to give *me* that.

The clangs of those thick sheets of metal slamming home have my lids peeling back.

Suitably shored up, defenses securely in place, I snag two plates, two bowls, and bring them over to the bags of Dragon Delight.

Then I grab silverware, forks and spoons for us, a ladle for the soup, big spoons I use specifically to serve up heaping portions of Dragon Delight—because there's no skimping when it comes to good food and there's definitely no skimping when it comes to wonton soup and lo mein and fried rice with chunks of perfectly sweet pork in it.

Only, I no sooner set that silverware down before Damon is moving close again. Near enough I can feel the heat from his body, but not so close that he's touching me. That buried longing in me pulses, desperate for his touch, threatening to slip free of the steel shielding. Especially when he says, "You really going to let me get away with saying that shit, Red?"

My heart starts beating faster, but I just lift my chin and glare at him. "You're here for reasons only known to you, and you're a stubborn fuck, so I know I don't have any hope of getting you to leave before you've accomplished what you came here to accomplish—"

His mouth quirks.

But I keep talking.

"In the meantime," I mutter, opening the container of soup and ladling some into my bowl—and doing it knowing I'm being selfish by taking the majority of the wontons, "I'm going to eat my food, drink my wine, and deal with it until you get it in your head to leave again."

Silence.

For long enough that I can't take it.

I look up from the mound of rice I've scooped onto my plate in the meantime.

He's studying me like I'm a puzzle he's never encountered before.

Then he's solving it and by doing so, he sends terror through me.

Because what Hiller did to me was traumatic. It haunted my nightmares and fucked up my life for months.

But he was far from the first person to hurt me—and he definitely didn't dole out the biggest wounds.

In fact, Hiller's violation was almost child's play when it comes to the rest of my life.

Especially my younger years.

"Who else left you, Red?" he asks, snapping me out of my swirling thoughts.

I open my mouth to lie, but then he lifts a hand, and I can't help it, I flinch away from the contact.

He sees that flinch—how could he not when it's right in front of him?—and moves even more slowly. But he doesn't stop. He keeps going, oh so slowly, until he's brushing the backs of his knuckles over my cheek. "Who else hurt you?"

Everything seizes in me again.

And so quickly, so fiercely that tears clog up in my throat and my eyes burn, the past swells up and—

No.

I'm not crying again.

Not over this shit.

I lift my chin, step away from his touch, and blatantly lie, "No one."

He tilts his head to the side and I brace, resist the urge to retreat.

I have to hold my ground. I have to steel myself in concrete and barbed wire and prepare for the impact of whatever bomb this man is going to drop on me.

Because it's all I know.

"No one hurt you," he says softly.

"Exactly." I drop the spoon back into the rice then reach for my bowl, my plate. "No one." Then I take advantage of his quiet to say, "Well, since you're here, we should talk about the team—"

"Nope."

I blink, surprise sliding through me.

Because if there's anything that Damon and I are comfortable with, it's talking about the team.

It's the safe spot.

It's where I'm most secure. Where the carefully constructed distance around him stays intact.

It's—

"No," he says as he starts loading up his plate, "we're not going to talk about the team."

"Um..." I blink again. "We're not?"

"Nope," he repeats, snagging my plate from my hand and moving over to the island, parking his ass on a stool, and setting my plate down at the spot next to him. "We're going to eat, and we're going to talk, and you're just going to deal, Red."

TEN

Damon

I WATCH the muscle flickering in her cheek for a long moment before she grabs her utensils, her bowl of wonton soup that's mostly wontons, and then stomps over to me.

"What?" she snaps. "We can't multitask—eat and talk about the team at the same time?"

"Nope," I tell her again. "Because we're not fucking talking about the team."

She freezes, halfway onto her stool.

Then I watch the steel gird her bones, grim determination come into her face. But, as I knew she would, she doesn't back down from the challenge in my words.

Instead, she finishes her assent, plunks that lush ass onto a stool, and glares at me.

But, a moment after that, the call of the wonton soup gets her and she starts eating.

Fuck, I like that about her.

She's not shy with her food, not worried that I'm going to judge her over what she's eating.

She just dives in.

But now I wonder how much of her always plowing forward is because she's running from the past.

"You going to stare at me?" she mutters through a mouth full of lo mein. "Or are you going to eat?"

So you can get the fuck out of here.

Though she leaves the last sentence unspoken, I sure as fuck don't miss the thought crossing through her mind.

And it has me fighting back a smile.

Considering that I don't want to end up with a fork protruding from one of my eyeballs, I stop staring and turn my focus to my own plate.

Fuck but Dragon is the best.

Who would think that high in the Sierra Nevadas there would be a kickass Chinese food restaurant?

I'm just happy to reap the rewards of that tonight.

And happy it means I won't have to hear Joey's stomach rumble again.

"I thought you said you were going to talk," she mutters after we've chowed down for several minutes.

This time I lose my fight with my smile. "No, Red. I said *we* were going to talk."

"Like *I* said"—it's still a mutter, but now it's a mutter bordering on a grumble—"I have some videos for you to review and—"

"And like *I* said—" I swivel in my stool, bend down until we're face to face—"we're not talking about the fucking team."

Her eyes narrow and I can see that she wants to ask what in the fuck all we're going to talk about then, but instead, she turns back to her plate.

I wait until she's consumed enough wonton soup that I deem it safe to speak again.

"You grew up in the Bay Area?"

She freezes, a wonton speared on her fork, the bite suspended an inch from her lips. "Yes," she says slowly before shoving the food in her mouth. "Why?" she asks as she chews and swallows.

"You grow up with your mom and dad?"

She sets the fork down, goes back to her spoon, and starts slurping broth. "Why?" she asks again.

Stubborn woman.

"Ky and I grew up in Maine with just our mom," I say, offering up shit I don't normally offer, but knowing it's a necessary evil, especially if I'm asking Joey to share. "Our dad skipped out when she was in diapers and I didn't hear fuck all from him until I got my first big paycheck in the league."

She jerks, eyes coming to mine.

And I see it—part of why I've kept my distance.

Because her siren's call of soft and steel makes me want to do everything I always promised myself I wouldn't do.

Claim a woman as my own.

Because that bastard is my father.

And because...I don't trust myself to—

"Ky is your sister?" she asks quietly and I clench my teeth together so sharply my jaw acts. Because I know she's thinking about the news stories, about how she and my sister endured similar awfulness at the hands of similarly awful men.

I nod. "Kylie."

"Older?" she asks. "Younger?"

"She's two years younger."

"Where is she now?"

"Here in town with me." I drop my fork onto my plate.

"After Mom died, she came to this coast and moved in a couple of months ago when she picked up a teaching gig."

Joey's head tilts to the side, that soft surpassing the steel. "What grade does she teach?"

"Seventh grade history." I chuckle. "For some reason, she's decided that her jam is corralling teenagers when they're objectively the most teenager-like."

"Seems to me that the trademark Connors backbone isn't afraid of a couple teenagers."

"Seems to me you'd be wrong." I chuckle again. "I helped her one day in class a couple of weeks back. Swear to fuck I've never sweated more, not even when I was playing in the league."

Joey giggles and it's such a rare sound, so light and sweet and *not* like steel that, for a moment, I'm frozen again, taking in the beauty of her amusement, of her smile, of the way her eyes dance. "It was really that bad?"

"It was worse." I snag my empty plate and hers, bring them both to the sink and start rinsing. "One kid told me I need to start moisturizing because I look scaly like a zoo snake."

There's silence.

But only for a heartbeat before she bursts out laughing.

And fuck if that isn't as beautiful as her giggle.

I go back for her now empty bowl, take it over to the sink, and load it in the dishwasher next to the plates and silverware.

She's still laughing by the time I make it back over to her, and I don't even give a fuck that it's at my expense.

She's laughing.

Not crying.

"I told Ky I'd never go back," I say solemnly, watching those green eyes dance.

"What?" she teases. "You're not going to start a moisturizing routine? Skin care is really important." Her brows flick up, eyes scanning my face. "*Especially* as we get older."

I frown at her, but inside I'm laughing too. "That was a weak roast, Red. You've been in locker rooms often enough—I know you can do better than that."

"I'm too content and full of Dragon Delight to truly put the work in."

Grinning, I climb back up onto my stool.

And I take advantage of the fact that she's relaxed enough to tease me by pressing for more information.

If I'm going to fill that emptiness inside her, I need to know everything.

"Tell me about your family, Red."

ELEVEN

Joey

IT'S A SNEAK ATTACK.

Such a gentle question after he got me to relax by being funny and cute that I'm not prepared.

I *should* have prepared.

I should have known this man wouldn't let this shit go.

"Seriously?" I mutter.

"You not wanting to share makes it seem like you lived with a bunch of serial killers."

They may as well have been.

They'd all but murdered my siblings.

The thoughts slide through my mind so quickly that I'm not prepared, that I don't have time to block them, to stop them from showing on my face.

Something I know he picks up on in an instant.

Screech!

My body jerks as he tugs my stool close to him, his legs

coming on either side of mine, one of his hands dropping to my waist, the other resting on the counter near my arm.

"What the fuck is that, Red?"

I inhale.

He's close, so close. And his deep blue eyes are fixed on mine, those golden flecks molten with rage. "What did they do to you?"

I don't want to talk about this shit.

I don't want to *think* about it.

But I also don't want to draw this argument out because I know Damon, I've experienced the recalcitrant asshole side of his personality many times over the last years, most recently last night. Hell, I experienced it thirty minutes ago on my back porch.

If I just say it, it'll be done and we can move on and never talk about it again.

"It's not so much as what they did, but what they *didn't* do," I say quietly. "We were homeschooled, my siblings—I was the oldest of four girls and a boy—and I. Which isn't bad in of itself. Plenty of people do it successfully. But my parents weren't educated themselves and they weren't consistent and they didn't do more than shove a workbook in our faces and expect us to magically educate ourselves." I sigh. "By the time I argued enough to be allowed to enroll in school, I was three grade levels behind in reading and four in math. My siblings didn't fare any better."

He nods, but doesn't speak, just lightly squeezed my hip.

There and listening.

Because he knows there's more.

And, unfortunately, there is.

"Because they weren't educated and because we didn't know better, we also weren't looked after in a lot of other ways. We lived off-grid and the water wasn't clean. We got sick a lot.

And none of us were vaccinated against any diseases, even though my parents were. So, when we brought chicken pox home from school, we were all pretty sick..."

This is where it gets harder.

I close my eyes for a second, shove down the memories.

So scared. Itching like a madwoman. Throwing up and shitting myself.

"And it was the combination of all of those things that killed my siblings," I force out, the words a rasp. "Chicken pox. Bad water that added to all of that sickness. And my parents not knowing better."

His fingers flex again.

"The twins died first. I woke up in the morning and went to check on them and..." I exhale, trying not to remember the horror of finding them. "Th-they were just gone," I whisper. "And my parents were out of their minds with grief. Charlotte and Ava were really sick too and even though I begged my parents to take them to the hospital they refused. They said the plants and honey we had would make them better."

Damon curses.

But I don't acknowledge it, acknowledge him or the pity in his eyes, the sadness in his frame.

I need to finish this.

"So, I packed the girls and I up, and I walked us all to the hospital."

A cold night.

A raging fever.

Stopping to puke and clean up my sisters.

Knowing we'd never make it.

And finally, finding a fire station.

"But we couldn't get there. It was four miles away and we'd only made two, so when I saw the fire station, I knew it was my only hope." An exhale. "But it was shut up tight, the lights off, no sign of anyone, but I banged on the door until one of the fireman came out. And then I passed out."

His fingers on the counter are drawn into a tight fist, the anger in his eyes a furious, terrifying thing.

I can't stop now, though.

"And when I finally woke up, days later, they were all gone." A beat. "It was just me left. I was fourteen," I whisper. "They were gone and I was too young, too fucking young to make it on my own."

"Of course you were," he whispers.

"My parents were there, wanted to take me home, but I didn't want to go. I refused actually, screamed and yelled until the doctors and nurses took pity on me and didn't go through with the discharge."

"Baby," he murmurs.

"I couldn't look at them." My throat works. "How could I fucking look at them? Live with them? *Love* them?"

"You couldn't," he says gently.

I nod in agreement. "I couldn't."

His hand on my side shifts, running lightly up and down my torso.

"Then the fireman who opened the door for us came into my room, and he fought for me." My voice breaks. "He was the *one* person who'd fought for me at that point. I went home with him. He and his wife healed me, brought me hockey, showed me what a real family could be like."

"He sounds like a great man."

"Yeah," I murmur. "He is. They both are. And now they're retired and touring the country with his wife, Beth. Last I heard, they were spending their days hiking in Arches National Park and then heading toward Zion."

That hand is still gently moving on my side. "You ever go with them?"

I shake my head. "Nah," I say. "I cramped their style for long enough. They deserve their freedom, not to be tied down with a kid they didn't want."

His brows drag together. "Why do you—"

But before he can finish the question—likely another one I don't want to answer—there's a knock at the door.

We both freeze.

"You expecting company?" he asks quietly.

I shake my head.

His eyes narrow, and he straightens, hops off the stool.

The loss of him close, of his warm, strong body hits hard, and thus, it takes me a second to process that this is my house and he's answering *my* door.

I climb down in a hurry, turn for the hall, and I've just reached the entryway when I hear,

"Who the hell are you?"

TWELVE

Damon

I'M STARING at the older couple on the porch, pieces clicking into place as I spot an RV parked at the curb.

But I don't so much as get a word out before the man, maybe early sixties with the beginnings of a beer belly and a handlebar mustache that doesn't fucking quit, barks, "Who the hell are you?"

I open my mouth again, but I don't get that out either.

Because the woman, petite and curved and wearing army green hiking pants, a cream long-sleeved tee, a sweater tied around her shoulders, looks beyond me and cries, "Josephine! My beautiful girl!"

Then she's pushing by me, hightailing it into the house like the ten feet between her and Joey is the best hike she's ever conquered, and the way she sweeps Joey into her arms for a long hug has our conversation flowing through my head again—knowing that she even keeps distance from these people who have love for her, who are protective.

Damn.

I don't have time to sit in that, though, because the man—who I figure must be the firefighter who saved her all those years ago—is showing his protective side.

He clears his throat, mustache twitching, cold eyes on mine. "I believe I asked you a question, son."

Immediately, my spine goes up.

I've never had patience for old codgers like this, who think their shit doesn't stink and that they're owed an explanation on their terms. My dad, when he popped back up in my life looking for a handout, had exactly the same demeanor and presumption.

But the reason this interaction doesn't send my rage spiraling is because this is the man who saved her.

Who protected her.

The man she clearly cares about.

So, I bite back the urge to snap back and just extend my hand. "Damon Connors."

His bushy brows pull together as he shakes it. "The GM?"

I nod. "Yes, Joey and I work together on the Sierra."

Instantly, his puffed-up demeanor melts away and he pumps my hand a few more times, mustache twitching again, but this time because he's smiling instead of scowling. "Joey speaks very highly of you, and we especially appreciate the quick action you took last season."

"Hiller is not only an asshole," I mutter, rage slicing through me, "but he's a fucking predator who deserves every bit of shit that's been shoveled onto him, *and* a whole lot more."

His smile grows and he breaks the handshake, clapping me on the shoulder. "Damn straight, son. Damn freaking straight."

He moves by me, walking down the hall, pausing by Joey and pulling her into a hug.

It doesn't last much longer than me closing and locking the

door, and by the time I reach them, he's drawing back. "Good to see ya, sweet pea."

"You too, John," she murmurs. "You—"

"Oh look!" I hear Beth cry. "Chinese! You don't mind if we join you guys, do you? I'm starved."

Joey glances at me, worry creeping into her eyes.

It's all empty.

My lungs go tight.

How are you going to make it better for her?

They go tighter.

Then all of that tightness just...relaxes.

Because there's yearning in Joey's eyes. She wants them here. She wants *me* here.

And...this is part of how I'm going to make it better, part of how I'm going to fill in that emptiness.

Simple as that.

I move into the kitchen, head straight for the cabinet with the dishes and pull out a couple more plates and bowls. "It might need a reheat," I tell Beth as I hand over one of the plates.

"That's okay, honey. It's been ages since I've had a meal I haven't had to cook in an RV kitchen. Just popping this plate into the microwave is a treat."

"Woman," John grumbles as he takes the other plate I hold out, "we just ate at that little Italian place you were begging me to stop at."

I set the bowls next to the container of soup and pause to take in the show.

Because Beth has dropped the spoon back into the rice and turned, plunking her hands on her hips. "That was *two* weeks ago!"

John starts scooping up rice, adding more to Beth's plate before heaping some onto his own. "Two weeks is an age?"

I glance up, see that Joey is having the same reaction I am.

The corners of her mouth are turned up.

I wink at her, watch as that tempting mouth curves up further.

Then I turn back to the show of John and Beth.

"When you're the one cooking breakfast, lunch, *and* dinner in a tiny RV kitchen then you'll know exactly how long two weeks is, dear."

He rolls his eyes. "It's fourteen days, honey bun."

"Okay"—she takes the fork I hold out without breaking stride—"then I'm off cooking duty. You fend for yourself."

A shrug. "So long as you empty the septic."

There's a blip of quiet. Then she lifts her chin, takes her plate to the counter, and turns to Joey. "We watched the game last night." She reaches out, snags Joey's hand. "Great job, honey."

"Notice she doesn't commit to emptying the tanks," John says in a stage-whisper.

I decide it's probably best to not comment on that. Instead, I nod toward the fridge. "What can I get you to drink? A beer?"

"Yeah, thanks," he says, taking his plate and sitting beside his wife.

The moment his ass hits the stool, Beth glares at him, but he ignores it, leans close, and presses his lips to hers. "Quit bitching," he mutters. "And I'll take you out for breakfast at the place you like in the morning."

"The one with the apple fritter pancakes?"

He nods. "If that's what you want, then that's what you'll get."

I'm watching them.

But I'm also watching Joey.

Seeing the softness in her face, the lightness in her smile, and...the longing in her eyes.

It's all empty.

How are you going to make it better for her?

I can't look away from those green eyes, from that naked longing, from...

What it calls to inside me.

I want that. I want to *give* her that. I want—

Panic slices through me.

Fuck. I can't do this.

I fucking *can't.*

"Son?" John calls and I jerk, my gaze tearing free of Joey. I glance over at him and he flicks up his brows. "You going to get me that beer?"

No. I'm going to get the fuck out of here, do everything in my power to take Joey and me back to how things were before.

It's all empty.

How are you going to make it better for her?

Those words slap hard across my consciousness, hard enough that I'm able to shove the panic down.

I inhale. Exhale.

Then I nod.

Turn to Beth.

"Would you like a beer too or something else to drink?"

THIRTEEN

Joey

"HE SEEMS NICE, HONEY," Beth says as we sit on my back deck.

Not long before, John kissed me on the top of the head, Beth on the lips, then slipped out to the RV, ready to consume his nightly dose of all things sports.

And Damon...well, he only left about ten minutes ago.

This was after he'd gotten John not just one beer, but three, and topped up Beth's glass of wine—and mine—several times.

It was after we demolished the peanut butter sundae pie and after Damon turned on the charm in a way I've never seen before—doing dishes, talking about what a good job I do with the team. He'd deflected most personal questions about himself, but I did learn that his mom's name was Darlene and he has an addiction to custom-made suits.

"He *is* nice," I say, somewhat surprising myself. Because I would have said Damon's predominate characteristics are grumpy, taciturn, and possessing a stubbornness that lives and breathes the sport and *only* the sport.

But nice?

No.

Only...that's how he was tonight.

And earlier. And last night.

Something that has me ignoring the flutter in my chest.

"But he's also my boss, Beth," I say. "So, don't get all romantic on me, yeah?"

"Oh, honey."

Her exasperated words have me glancing toward her. She's shaking her head, lips turned up at the edges. "What?" I ask.

"The *what* is that you're trying to tell me you haven't noticed the way he looks at you."

The flutter in my chest comes back, *grows.*

"Beth," I say. "He's my boss."

"Not really, though," she points out and she's not completely right, but she's also not completely wrong. "Don't the owners and the board have the ultimate say about your job?"

"Yes, but they take Damon's opinion seriously."

Case in point, me having the head coaching job in the first place.

"Hmm," Beth murmurs. "I'm sure that's true." She sips from her wine then turns and smiles at me. "Still, I like the way he looks at you."

I do too.

It's the fantasy I've been harboring for years.

And yet, I know, at the end of the day, it means nothing.

"He's protective," I say, shrugging. "You know that things were tough with Hiller—"

She scowls fiercely, and my heart squeezes. While she doesn't know the whole story of what happened to me—no one except Damon does—I've told her and John enough for them to understand exactly how toxic it was behind the scenes.

Plus, she knows what happened to Ivy and the others because that's why I'm in the position I'm in.

Her words that follow are just as fierce as her scowl. "I hope that asshole rots in prison for the rest of his sorry life."

I doubt he will.

Because the world doesn't seem to punish men who hurt women.

"Damon's sister was hurt by a man," I tell her, not wanting to share the details of a story that's not mine to tell, and even though it was in the news, I'm not sure Beth is up to date on old hockey scandals, about my boss or not. "He's protective of the women around him is all. It's nothing more than that."

It feels like more.

But that's not Damon.

It's not Damon and me.

It's just...*not*.

I feel her gaze on me but deliberately keep my eyes on my wine glass.

Thankfully, she doesn't push me. Well, she *does* say, "I think you may be wrong about that, honey," but that's quickly followed by, "Do you have time to come to brunch with us before you coach tomorrow?"

"For apple fritter pancakes?" I glance up, smiling at her. "I'll make the time. Do you guys want to come to the game? Or will you be back on the road?"

Her mouth quirks. "We already bought our tickets."

"Beth!" I admonish. "You know I could have gotten you some."

She lifts a shoulder, drops it. "More ticket sales mean that our favorite girl is more likely to keep doing her dream job."

"Dammit," I whisper.

"What?" she asks.

I wave my hand in front of my face. "No fair making me teary-eyed."

"Dammit," *she* whispers.

"What?" I ask, blinking rapidly.

"No fair making *me* teary-eyed."

John and Beth never had kids—they couldn't—and they put their retired life and dreams of traveling the US on hold until I was done with college.

I'll never be able to repay them for that.

I reach out and take her hand. "I hope you're aware of exactly how much I appreciate and care for you guys."

"Honey," she rasps out, fingers spasming around mine, her other hand waving in front of her face as she blinks rapidly. "No fair giving me more teary-eyeness."

I grin. "You're tough. You can handle it."

She grins back. Then her face softens. "You brought so much joy and pride and *love* into our lives."

I close my eyes, the words wrapping around my heart and squeezing tightly. "Beth," I whisper.

"I love you, honey," she murmurs. "I know the old codger and I don't say it often enough, but we do."

"I love you too."

She sniffs.

I sniff.

"Oh geez," I hear John say as he comes out onto the back porch. "Not this again."

"John!" she snaps. "Joey and I were having a moment and you ruined it!"

He tugs lightly on my ponytail, smiling at me.

And I know he loves me too.

I can see it in his eyes.

Then he's sitting down in the empty chair next to Beth and

me and I'm asking them about their trip, listening to them banter (a.k.a. argue), and it's like that time when I lived with them. They loop me in without it feeling awkward, even when I'm sitting back in my chair and just watching them act like the lovable lunatics they are.

We talk late into the night about everything and nothing and I think...

Well, I think some part of that gnawing emptiness inside me is filled in.

Only, after they've gone off to bed in their RV, after I've taken a bath and crawled beneath my own covers, I know it's only temporary.

Because that's when the emptiness creeps back in.

FOURTEEN

Damon

"I LOVE HOCKEY," Kylie says, her smile wide as she loads up a plate from the spread in one corner of the box.

"Since when?" I mutter. "You haven't been to a game in years."

"I did my time growing up." She punches me lightly on the shoulder. "And let me say, those youth games did *not* have this kind of spread."

"Which means you don't love hockey. You love *snacks*," I correct, bumping my shoulder against hers before I reach over and snag a bottle of water.

"You say potato..."

My lips twitch, but I just twist open the lid on the bottle then move over to the seats that overlook the rink.

Warmups are done. The Zamboni has cleaned the ice. Anthems have been sung and the players have filled their requisite benches, five on each side taking their places on the ice.

Puck drop is imminent.

Which means I need to sit my ass in this chair and watch the players below do what I dream of.

What I lost.

What I'll never have again.

I don't regret what I did.

I do regret the fact that I haven't stepped foot on the ice since—first because my contract was voided, then because I was on house arrest. I was lucky I had to do very little actual jail time, though still more than the asshole who hurt Kylie. And anyway, by the time I even thought about strapping on my skates again, it was too painful to get back into that headspace again.

Luckily, I had still had connections in the league.

I got a gig scouting then assisting with player development and eventually was an assistant GM for a few years before I came here.

Before I inherited something that was a hidden nightmare.

The crowd quiets and the whistle trills, players moving into position for the puck drop.

A moment later, the game is under way.

Lake wins the puck back to Riggs on defense and we're off, moving into the offensive zone, gaining entry, getting a legitimate shot on net before play swings back the other way and we're on the defensive.

It's back and forth for long minutes, the crowd oohing and aahing, gasping and cheering in equal turn, and by the end of the first we're still scoreless.

That's okay.

That's hockey.

Sometimes it's a game of patience.

Sometimes it's a grind.

Sometimes it's a brutal battle until something good happens.

Like toward the end of the second when Storm tips a shot and sends it sailing into the upper corner of the net.

The crowd erupts, but my gaze is drawn to the bench and I feel Joey's wide grin in my gut. She nods at Storm as he skates back to the bench, turns to Dave, our offensive coach, and tells him something that has him making a note on his tablet.

Then, just that quickly, the smile is gone and she's focused, back to business.

"How's that going?"

I flick my eyes to Kylie then back out at the ice. "Considering the guys just scored, it's going pretty well."

"With Joey," she admonishes gently.

"It's been two days since you and I talked, kid."

She lifts and drops one shoulder in a careless shrug. "When has that ever stopped you before?"

"Ky," I warn.

A warning she completely ignores.

"You're Damon," she murmurs. "You had a plan even before we finished the conversation."

I turn my gaze back out to the ice, to the game, but I'm not actually seeing what's happening, not processing or analyzing anything below.

I'm thinking about my plan to fill that emptiness in Joey.

I'm thinking about John and Beth and the obvious love they have for her—love she doesn't seem to see or accept.

I'm thinking about what she told me, all she's endured.

And yeah, I fucking have a plan.

I just wish it didn't scare me fucking shitless.

After the game, Kylie and I head for the elevators.

I need to stop by my office and grab some shit for the road

trip coming up in a couple of days and since I'm the pipsqueak's ride, she's stuck tagging along.

But when the doors open and we step off, I hear voices that surprise me.

"Look at this place, John!" Beth exclaims. "It's so fancy!"

"It's a hallway and some pictures, Beth," John mutters. "It's hardly the Ritz."

Kylie chokes, and I glance over at her.

"Um," she whispers, brows flying up.

But before I can explain, Beth spots us and rushes over. "Damon! Oh, my gosh! This place is so lovely!"

"Um," Kylie whispers again, eyebrows lifting somehow higher.

"And, oh, my gosh"—she turns to Ky and grasps both of her hands—"you're lovely too."

"This is my sister, Kylie," I say by way of introduction. "And, Ky, this is Beth, Joey's mom."

Something comes over Beth's face, an acute kind of pain mixed with joy. Then she tucks that away, squeezes Kylie's hands. "So nice to meet you, Kylie."

I know my sister didn't miss that expression either when she says gently, "It's nice to meet you too, Beth. Did you guys watch Joey coach?"

Beth's smile widens, but it's John who answers. "Damn right we did." He sticks his hand out. "John."

Kylie shakes it. "She did great."

John nods, mustache twitching when he grins and says, "Damn right she did."

Ky's eyes are dancing when she glances up at me, but before she can reply, I see a flash of red and look to the side as Joey turns the corner. She's in a snug button down and slacks and my dick twitches at the sight of those lean curves.

Her eyes widen slightly at the sight of us all gathered near the elevators and she pauses for a heartbeat before continuing toward us.

"Hey guys," she says, leaning in and squeezing Beth first then John. "Did you have fun?"

"We had the best time!" Beth exclaims. "You did so good, honey!"

"There were a lot of people," John grumbles. "But you did good, Joey."

"Thanks." The moment stretches before she hitches a thumb over her should. "Well, I should"—her eyes flick between me and Kylie, Beth and John—"get back. I'll see you guys in the morning before you head out on the road again?"

"Do you know Damon's sister, Kylie?" Beth blurts.

"Oh," Joey says gently, gaze drifting to mine, holding for a second, then sliding on as though she expected a different answer, as though she thought Kylie was another woman and she was *jealous*.

Why do I like that so much?

Because I'm an asshole.

"It's nice to meet you, Kylie." She sticks her hand out for Ky to shake.

"You too," Kylie replies with a smile.

"I know!" Beth claps her hands together, the glee on her face sending my stomach sinking. "Kylie, you and Damon should join us for brunch tomorrow."

"I—" Joey and I both begin at the same time.

And then stop, glancing at each other, knowing that we're both thinking the same exact thing.

No.

No fucking way.

But the pause gives Kylie enough time to join in with Beth's maneuvering.

"I love brunch!"

She does.

Mostly, she loves mimosas.

And she knows that I won't deny her something she loves.

"I—" Joey begins again.

But Beth and Kylie are off and running, planning the restaurant—one that I can't deny is really good—and the time—late enough that we'll all get enough sleep, but early enough they'll be able to navigate the RV out of the mountains before the sun sets.

"I—"

"That works perfectly!" Beth says once the details are confirmed. "I'm looking forward to talking to you more," she adds conspiratorially, winking at my sister.

"You too," Kylie says just as conspiratorially.

And hell, she winks back.

I glance at Joey, know her wide eyes mirror mine.

Same as I know...

We're in trouble.

FIFTEEN

Joey

"OH, THAT LOOKS ABSOLUTELY DELICIOUS!" Beth exclaims as the waitress sets the plate of fluffy buttermilk pancakes topped with whipped cream and caramelized bananas in front of her.

She's not wrong.

It looks amazing.

Though mine—topped with Nutella and strawberries and those gorgeous mounds of whipped cream—looks better.

"It *looks* like a sugar coma," John grumbles. "All three of you."

Because Kylie got pancakes too—hers topped with lemon curd and whipped cream.

"Carbs fuel your brain," she says without missing a beat and I can't help but like her, can't help but admire her exuberance and the joy for life that just exudes out of her.

Not gonna lie, though, I'm a little jealous of Kylie Connors.

She's Beth but forty years younger—bright and joyous and with a dash of mischief thrown in.

Case in point? She ignores John's scowl and cuts off a humungous piece of pancake with her fork, plunking it into her mouth, eyes dancing as she moans, "Mmm. Sugar."

I bite back a giggle, turn and see that Damon has an indulgent smile on his face.

Sweet.

Loved.

My heart twinges.

Because someone hurt her, left wounds—my stomach clenches—that will never be healed. It's proof the world is fucked up. Proof that good doesn't always triumph over bad.

I wonder where she hides her wounds, wonder if Damon somehow managed to heal them.

But I have my doubts.

It's not so simple...

Only when I look back at her, see the bond, the love that she and Damon share, I think that maybe sometimes miracles *do* happen.

That Damon might have superpowers.

That I might be healed too—if I only let him in.

My pulse speeds up and I clench my fork tighter. Damon's superpowers don't matter. I have so many wounds that the ones Hiller left me barely track.

And yeah, maybe that's a lie I tell myself.

But it's also not far from the truth.

Better to hurt me than someone else.

I can take it.

But...why do I have to?

That question hits me hard, hits me hard enough that I glance down at my pancakes and don't feel a lick of hunger.

Nope. That's disappeared like a whiff of smoke.

"You gonna stare at those pancakes all day?" John asks gruffly. "Or you gonna eat before it gets cold?"

I pick up my fork and take a bite, but I barely taste it.

I still force a smile, still answer, "Delicious," when Beth asks me if it's good.

The waitress comes back and deposits Damon's egg white scramble with extra veggies and John's oatmeal in front of each of them.

But Damon doesn't start eating.

He's watching me, staring at me.

Seeing me.

Quickly, I drop my gaze back to my pancakes.

And I start shoveling them into my mouth even though I might as well be eating sawdust.

Eventually, I choke down enough of my meal for it to not be noticeable that my stomach is churning, smiling at all the right places as Beth and Kylie chatter, chiming in when necessary. I know I should be enjoying this, should be soaking it all in and holding it close for later.

I don't see Beth and John enough.

This is a luxury I should revel in.

But I can't.

God, I'm so messed up.

So broken and empty and...

Pathetic.

Luckily, I don't have time to think about that for long because Damon slips away and takes care of the bill—before John and I can argue over who'll pay it—and much grumbling ensues, by both John and me. Meanwhile, Beth and Kylie keep chatting through it, the lights inside them not dimmed in the least as we all pile out of the restaurant.

Then...it's time to say goodbye.

Beth hugs me tightly enough that my lungs protest, and

then she's stepping back, giving way to John, who draws me close and kisses me on the cheek. "Keep up the good work, kiddo."

"I will."

He smiles at me then turns to Damon, sticking out a hand as Beth and Kylie hug. I watch as the latter two whisper something in each other's ears then exchange numbers while the former pair just nod brusquely at each other.

Damon steps back and holds my eyes for a long moment.

But before I can figure out a pithy reply, he turns and walks away, Kylie trailing behind him.

And then I stand there as Beth and John do the same, loading up into their RV and slowly pulling out of the lot.

Leaving me alone.

Again.

Always.

I zip my suitcase closed and straighten, setting it on the floor and rolling it down the hall.

It's early. We play tomorrow but we're flying out today in order to give the guys time to settle into the hotel for a good night's sleep tonight, along with padding the schedule in case of any weather delays or other hiccups in our travel schedule.

I didn't sleep well last night.

Two days with Beth and John weren't enough, especially with work in between, but it was also too much, reminding me of...

Too many things.

Add in Damon and Kylie, brunch and wine and crying jags and sharing far too much and allowing far too many emotions to run free...and these last few days have sat heavy on my brain.

"Coffee," I mutter.

I need caffeine and to shove all of that out of my head.

We have eighty more games this season, and if I keep doing this shit it's going to feel even longer.

I need to keep my focus, need to do my job, need to—

The doorbell rings.

I jump, gaze jerking to the window over the sink, the still-lightening dawn sky dimly shining through the glass.

Too early for solicitors.

And Beth and John aren't popping in for another surprise visit.

That leaves—

My stomach lurches as the doorbell goes again.

I grab my phone, pull up the camera app, and—

My belly churns for a completely different reason this time.

Damon is standing on the stoop. Again.

I exhale, slap a lid on all the things I'm feeling, then move to answer the door.

"Damon," I say, "is everything okay?"

He steps toward me and I have no choice but to back up—it's either that or stand there and let him run into me. When he's cleared the door, he reaches behind him and shuts it, the lock clicking closed with a soft *snick*.

"What's going on?" I ask.

He jerks his head to the kitchen, starts walking that way before I can get an answer.

When I make it into the kitchen, he's already helping himself to a cup of coffee—pouring two mugs before lifting one to his lips and drinking deeply.

"Make yourself at home, why don't you?" I mutter, marching forward and taking the cup he holds out, drinking deeply, feeling the rough edges of sleep being sanded away.

Once I've drank half the mug down I look back up at him, see him smiling. "What?" I ask, my tone still a little sharp.

"Now you're awake," he says and sets his cup down.

"What?" I ask again, brows furrowing.

He nods to my suitcase. "That everything you're bringing?"

My frown deepens. "That and my backpack..." But I don't finish the thought because he's moving to the table where my knapsack is, snagging it and my suitcase. "What are you—?"

But then he's striding for the hall, tossing over his shoulder, "Finish your coffee." A beat.

"Then we need to head to the airport."

SIXTEEN

Damon

THE TENSION IS rampant in my car as I drive, thick enough I can cut it with a knife.

I ignore it and just drive steadily through the curved roads leading down from Joey's place and out toward the airport.

The guys meet at the practice rink and take the bus over, but there's enough parking that Joey and I usually park directly at the private airfield itself. Of course, usually Joey and I drive separately.

Hence the tension.

"Gonna clue me in why you've kidnapped me and my luggage?"

"Don't think I can actually kidnap luggage." I glance over at her when I feel the tension ratchet tighter. "Just saying."

She rolls her eyes. "*Just saying,* gonna clue me in as to why you've kidnapped me and *stolen* my luggage?"

I focus back on the road, mouth curving. "Nope."

There's a long blip of quiet.

Then she asks archly, "*Nope?*"

I flick my gaze to hers before looking forward again. "Yup," I say. "Nope."

The silence descends a second time, for long enough that the airport appears in the distance. But thankfully her impatience arrives before the turnoff for the parking lot. "Damon," she says softly. "What the hell are you doing?"

"I told you."

She exhales sharply. "No, you haven't. You got a bee in your bonnet"—my mouth curves because that's funny as fuck—"about something that shouldn't matter to you."

I react before I stop to think, jerking the wheel, pulling us over to the shoulder and spinning in my seat, glaring down at her. "It shouldn't matter to me?" I growl, leaning toward her. "It shouldn't fucking *matter?*"

"Look." She leans back, rubbing a hand over her forehead, but I don't miss that as she pushes the hair out of her face, she takes the opportunity to lean back, to put some distance between us.

That pisses me off even more.

She shouldn't be putting distance between us.

She should be shifting closer, reaching out—

Fuck.

Enough.

"Look what?" I press.

"My life is my own life," she says, dropping her hand and lifting her chin. "You were a pushy fuck and I shared shit that no one aside from my therapist knows. I get that triggered some hero complex in you, but I don't need you to rescue me, Damon. I fucking *don't.*"

"Empty," I say.

She blinks. "What?"

"You said you were empty."

"I'm fine."

"You're a fucking liar," I tell her.

"Damon!"

"But I don't care." I check for traffic then pull out onto the road.

"You don't care?" she grinds out.

"Nope," I say. "I don't care if you say you're fine. You're not. You're fucking empty and I'm going to change that shit. I'm going to fill you up, Red."

"Why? Because you have some sort of fucked-up White Knight Complex?" She laughs humorlessly. "I'm not some weakling who needs to be saved."

"Trying to piss me off?" I ask, even though the sharp edges of my temper have me clenching my steering wheel tightly. "It's not going to work."

"It doesn't normally take much."

She's not wrong.

My patience is shit and my temper is finely honed to a sharp point, ready to explode at all times.

"True. But I understand now."

"No," she snaps. "What you mean is that hearing the shit that happened to me brought up some big feelings in you. But I'm not your sister, Damon."

I suck in a breath, that slender hold I always have on my temper slipping, threatening to fracture, to allow that barbed edge loose, free to cause hurt.

She's still talking though.

And that's the only reason I manage to rein it in.

"I'm not weak," she says caustically. "Life is fucked. Shit goes wrong. Bad stuff happens to innocent people. But I don't let it drag me down. I fucking *can't*. And you continuing to act like I'm some princess perched in a tower that needs rescuing doesn't help. It makes it infinitely harder for me to stay focused.

I need to stay in my lane, to stay focused, to be the best at my job as I can."

"There's more to life than hockey."

She laughs again and it's as sharp as my temper.

As brittle as my control.

"That's rich coming from you."

I scowl before I can stop myself. "Joey," I warn.

"What?" She makes a frustrated sound. "You don't like me pointing out your hypocrisy?"

But there's a thread in her voice.

Victory.

Like she knows she's pushed me to a breaking point...and thus pushed me away.

My hold on my temper turns to steel. I shove my frustration down, ignore her question—and maybe the realization that she's not wrong. "Yes," I say. "Bad shit happens to good people. But I don't see you as a woman who needs rescuing."

She sniffs. "Right." It's a dry rejoinder. "Sure."

"Red—"

"And *you* trying to lecture me on the fact that there's more to life than hockey." Another sniff. "That's fucking rich."

I pull into a spot but don't put the transmission into park because that will unlock the doors and I don't want Joey to be able to escape, not quite yet anyway. "I have a life, baby," I tell her gently. "I have friends and I have my sister. I work a lot, but it's not the only thing in my world. I go out to dinner, grab a drink with one of my buddies, go to see shitty movies with my sister. Can you say the same?"

I know the answer to that, even before she turns her irate gaze to mine.

It's a no.

Because she goes to Sierra games, she goes to practice, she watches video and makes plans for the team and basically lives and breathes doing everything she can to make the organization the best it can be.

But there are no Game Nights or bad movies or drinks with friends—no matter the city we're in.

There's no shopping days or trips to the spa.

There's no planned meetups with Beth and John, no treating herself to a nice dinner with some girlfriends.

It's...empty.

And I know that she's used to it.

I know that she, for some reason, thinks she deserves it.

And I know that she fucking *hates* it, even as she wears it like it's the mantle she must bear.

Same as I know I can't let that truth stand.

Not for another day, another hour, another fucking *second*.

But I also know that today's not the day that truth is going to stick.

"You can't," I say, shifting into park.

Not a second after the locks disengage, she pops open the door, letting in the cold morning air.

"Fuck you," she hisses.

She slams it shut, moves to the trunk, and a moment later, I watch her, with her backpack perched on her shoulders, wheel her suitcase across the tarmac.

Then I smile.

Because mad isn't distant.

Because buried longing isn't unaffected.

And because...nothing good is ever easy.

SEVENTEEN

Joey

I'M TUCKED AWAY in the corner of the hotel bar, giving the guys who're unwinding with a beer the space to relax without their coach watching them.

Lines are prepped for tomorrow, reports on our affiliate teams are in. There are a couple of young players I'm watching, seeing when they might be ready to come up and play in The Show. But they're not quite there yet.

Soon though.

Someone will be sick or injured or just need a rest day to prevent an injury, and they'll get their shot.

My work is done.

I need to go up to bed.

But I'm delaying, knowing that I'm just going to lay there, staring up at the ceiling.

Thinking about Damon.

Ugh.

Dumb as hell. I sigh, down the rest of my beer, and start

gathering my papers. There's nothing to be done about it. I'll take a long bath, do my best to turn into a prune, and hopefully the soak will make me drowsy enough to drift off.

Not likely.

But we have a skate in the morning and the game in the evening. If I'm not tired enough to sleep tonight, I'll definitely drop off tomorrow night.

Exhaustion for the win.

I shove everything in my bag, start to toss it over my shoulder.

Only, I don't make it that far.

Damon's there.

My heart flutters before I have a chance to lock it down.

And then he's tossing my bag over *his* shoulder and turning around, saying, "Come on, Red."

I blink. Once. Then twice.

But he's walking away, weaving through the tables and chairs like he doesn't have a care in the world.

Hell, maybe *he* doesn't.

But I'm getting really fucking tired of him giving me an order and just expecting me to follow.

Of course, I can't do anything about that right now. He's already in the freaking lobby, heading for the elevators, and... my freaking room key is in the bag he commandeered.

"Fucking hell," I mutter.

But I follow.

Because I have no fucking choice.

I reach him just as the elevator doors slide open with a soft ding. He glances down at me, half his mouth hitched up, then lifts a hand, indicating I should precede him.

"You're an asshole, you know that?" I mutter as I step on.

The other half of his mouth curves. "Not something I don't already know."

He jabs at a button and since it's my floor, I don't comment.

I just keep scowling at him.

"I see you got those walls locked down tight, baby," he murmurs as we start heading up.

My scowl deepens.

He chuckles, but he doesn't say anything further. Maybe because he's an asshole, but probably because the doors have opened and he's walking down the hall.

I have no choice but to follow.

Something that's even more annoying.

He turns the corner, moves to the end of the hall, and swipes a keycard.

I pause beside him, hold out my hand. "Give me my bag."

He doesn't answer me, just pushes inside his room.

And again, I have no choice but to follow.

Maybe I'll smother him with a pillow, put us both out of our misery.

Then I sigh, allow the door to close behind me, lean back against it. He doesn't stop moving, though. Just walks through the room, pulls at the handle on the sliding glass door, and steps outside, taking my bag with him.

"What the fuck?" I whisper.

I stand there for a moment then I follow him onto the balcony.

"First of all," I say as I step through the door, "why the fuck do you get a balcony?"

He sets his bag in the far corner, turns back toward me, his smile a flash of white in the darkness. "Perks of being the big boss." He settles in a chair—conveniently between me and my bag—and rests his feet on the banister. "Take a load off, Red."

I exhale and it's a frustrated sound.

One I know he picks up on because his mouth curves.

But he doesn't move.

And he doesn't speak.

And, eventually, I huff out another frustrated sigh and sink down into the other chair.

"You're feeling vulnerable," he says after another long moment.

He's not wrong. Not that I'm going to admit it—not even under pain of torture.

Which...this conversation is.

"I got a glimpse behind the curtain," he goes on. "I saw shit you didn't want me to see, and now you're desperate to put walls up."

"It's amusing that you're talking about walls when you have the strongest set of concrete and barbed wire barriers erected around yourself that I've ever seen."

He lifts and drops one shoulder in a careless shrug. "Maybe I don't have those anymore."

I sniff.

"Or maybe it's that I don't have them with *you*."

My heart squeezes. "That's not true." Still, I can't shove down the hope blooming in my belly.

Screech!

My body jerks as he drags my chair closer to his.

"Stop doing *that*. It's really freaking annoy—"

Then his face is in mine, blue eyes blazing. "You want the truth?"

"I..." My throat is tight but I manage to squeeze out, "What do you mean?"

He leans closer, one hand lifting, pressing lightly to my cheek. "Do you want the truth of why I've always avoided this?"

"Avoided what?"

His eyes grow hotter. His impatience grows. "Avoided

being alone with you, avoided anything that wasn't professional, avoided anything that would bring me closer to you."

My lungs spasm. "Why do you mean?"

"I know you want me," he murmurs. "I've seen it in your eyes, felt it in your body, and part of the reason it's so damned hard to keep my distance.

"But you've come over to my house," I whisper.

"The other coaches were there," he says. "And when they weren't, there was always something I had to get back to, most often Kylie, who I wouldn't blow off."

No, he wouldn't.

"I stayed away because I didn't trust myself. Because I knew I couldn't be open to something with you. It's irresponsible. It pushes boundaries I shouldn't push. And I knew I couldn't be the man you deserved, the man you needed. I'm too broken, too damaged, too closed down, too dangerous—"

"Damon—"

"But from the first time I saw you," he says, talking over me, "I wanted you. Then I got to know you and I wanted you more. And yeah I told myself what you needed was anyone but me, yeah I know I'm not good for you. But then you told me you were empty, baby—"

I inhale sharply.

His fingers flex on my jaw. "You shared what you shared and you told me you were *empty*."

My exhale is just as sharp.

"And so...everything changed."

EIGHTEEN

Damon

CHRIST, I've been delusional.

Thinking I could stay away.

Thinking I could somehow fix all this shit for her and keep my distance.

Could stay just friends.

When I dream about her most every night. When I think about her far too often during the day. When I—

"Damon," she whispers then asks when my eyes come to hers, "What changed?"

"You gave me you."

Her eyes go wide. "No, I didn't. I shared some shit that happened to me because you're a pushy asshole—"

I shake my head. "That's not the right story, Red."

Her eyes go even wider. "Damon—"

"You're scared."

"Damn right, I am." She waves a hand down her front. "I'm a mess inside and nobody needs to—"

I lean in, press my forehead to hers. "You're not a mess. You're strong and beautiful and smart and talented and—"

"Stop," she whispers.

"No," I tell her. "You're a good person and you've been through so much and you're still here, baby. You're still fighting and thriving and—"

"*Stop.*"

"I couldn't protect my sister and went off half-cocked, beating up that guy, paying the price for it, but that doesn't change the fact that I didn't protect her in the first place."

"Damon—"

"But you, baby, you tried to save them even though you were fighting for your own life—"

"I didn't, and I didn't protect the women on the team." Her voice breaks and she leans back. "If I had, things would have been different and Ivy and the others wouldn't have—"

"You were scared and hurt, baby. You did what you could."

She shakes her head, pushes away from me, shoulders slumping as she whispers, "I don't want to talk about this anymore. I don't want to talk about the past anymore. It's over and there's nothing I can do to change it."

I can give her that play.

If we keep digging at the wounds of our pasts they'll never heal.

And I don't want her to hurt anymore.

"Okay, baby," I say softly. "Then what *do* you want to talk about?"

"What if I said that I didn't want to talk at all?" She leans in, hand settling on my chest, drifting lower.

My dick goes hard in an instant, but I catch her hand before it can get there.

"Red"—I press a kiss to her palm—"I didn't bring you here for this."

"I know." Her mouth curves. "But I've dreamed about it for a long time. Will you..." Her lips press flat then release, reddening those plump lips of hers. "Will you give that to me?" she whispers. "Will you fill me up?"

Christ, this is dangerous as fuck.

All of it.

From showing up on her porch to hanging out with Beth and John to bringing her to my room, all of it is dumb as hell. But the constant push-pull of want and doing what's right is—

It's all empty.

How are you going to make it better for her?

I can't keep it up any longer—the distance, the keeping my needs in check, doing the right thing because it's the right thing.

So I finally...just give in.

Weaving my fingers into her hair, I tilt her head back. Wide green eyes. Pink cheeks. Kissable lips.

Gorgeous heart.

I lower my mouth to hers and the first touch of her lips against mine is electric.

Damn.

That's not good for my control, not at fucking all.

And when, a moment later, she moans softly, lips parting to allow me in to taste her, it's even worse for my fragile hold on it.

My dick is aching. Sweat has broken out on my spine. My nose is full of the soft scent of her, the silk of her hair settles over my hand. I need to feel her body against mine, need to stroke the curves of her, need to taste them.

But she's two steps ahead of me.

She places both of her hands against my chest and shoves hard enough that I'm almost dumped out of my chair. The next second, she's on her feet, grabbing my hand, dragging me up too.

I snag her bag and then we're inside the room, bag on the

ground, slider closed, my hands all over that gorgeous body. It feels like everything I've dreamed of—soft and feminine and *mine*.

"Damon," she whispers, her hands kneading at my shoulders, drawing me closer, lips parting.

And I can't resist the invitation.

I bend, take her mouth, meeting the thrusts of her tongue, driving my hand into her hair again, tilting her head back and tasting her exactly how I've dreamed of.

"Bed," she murmurs. "Hurry."

"No."

She jerks, eyes going wide, the haze of pleasure fading, concern and embarrassment weaving through expression.

I gently tuck her hair behind her ear. "We're not going to hurry, Red."

Those eyes go wider.

"We're going to take it slow, going to squeeze every bit of pleasure out of tonight we can."

Lips parting, emerald eyes going somehow wider.

"I'm going to learn every inch of your body, learn what makes you squirm and what makes you blush and what makes you"—I slide my hand down her belly, slipping one finger into the waistband of her slacks, brushing it lightly over the silken skin there—"*wet*."

Her inhale is sharp.

"And if you don't like something, if we go too far or too fast or you just change your mind"—I cup her jaw—"all you have to do is just say the word, baby. We'll stop, no matter how far we've gone and there will be no questions asked."

She goes still, not breathing for so long that I say, "Breathe, baby."

She exhales.

And I see it, that look that used to bring terror to every part of me—because I couldn't risk falling for someone, because if something bad happened and I wasn't there to stop it, because if my hold on my temper snapped and *I* was the one to inflict hurt...

How could I fucking live with myself.

But right now it's not fear I'm feeling.

Right now, it makes me feel a hundred feet tall.

"Damon," she whispers and her next question hits me hard, "Are you sure? This— Us—" Her eyes close for a moment then reopen. "You made it pretty clear before that you didn't want—"

"I've *always* wanted."

Her fingers flex on my shoulders.

"Always," I repeat. "I'm not convinced I'm good for you. I'm not convinced that I can give you what you need. I'm not convinced I can trust myself with you—"

She frowns.

"But"—I swipe my thumb lightly along her cheek, tracing the edge of the flush there—"I'm also not convinced that knowing all I do about you, knowing how beautiful and smart and funny and sweet you are...I'm not convinced I can stay away any longer, baby."

NINETEEN

Joey

I DON'T FEEL EMPTY.

In fact, I feel so full that I'm overflowing.

I need to say something profound, something that can match what his words have brought to me, but I've got nothing.

This isn't a motivational speech in a locker room, hyping the guys up so they kick some ass on the ice.

This is...my life.

This is dangerous and probably stupid and will likely leave me more shattered than I've ever been before.

Because I want it so much that I can taste it, feel it, *love* it.

And that's a drug I can't resist.

So, instead of calling this, instead of snagging my bag and making my retreat, I answer his quiet admission of not being able to stay away with, "Then don't."

The air goes taut.

His blue eyes darken with desire.

Then he *moves*.

One hand diving into my hair, tilting my head back again, the other going to my waist. One tug has my body flush against his and I gasp because the feel of him—hard and male and so damned strong—makes my knees wobble.

"Too much?" he murmurs, head dropping, lips lightly brushing my earlobe as he speaks.

"No," I say softly. "It's good." A beat. "And not nearly enough."

His mouth whispers along my jaw, drifting close to my lips. "What about this?" His tongue darts out. "Is it too much?" he asks, the hot puffs of his words glazing my skin.

"No, sweetheart." My head drops back when he moves to my neck, mouth lightly pressing to my skin, the bristles of his beard the most erotic sort of tease. Because of that, it takes me a moment to realize he's gone still. "Damon?" I ask, starting to lift my head again.

His fingers tighten in my hair and his lips start moving again. "Like that, baby."

"Like wh-what?" I manage as goose bumps rise on my flesh, as my knees wobble, as desire swirls rapidly through my insides.

"You calling me sweetheart."

My hands clench on his shoulders, surprise sliding through me.

Badass, grumpy, taciturn Damon Connors who doesn't need anyone else likes being called *sweetheart?*

The rush of emotions inside me is so strong that I wonder how I'll stand it.

But I don't have time to sit in those feelings—or the panic that hurtles in behind them.

Because he kisses me.

And I've never had a kiss like this—lazy and unhurried and yet steadily driving me higher and higher, closer to the edge of insanity.

Or maybe toward needing to have him naked and on top of me and pounding hard and deep and—

"Too much?" he rasps as he breaks away and reaches for the buttons on my shirt, undoing one.

"Still not enough."

His mouth quirks.

Then he undoes another button before dropping his head and flicking out his tongue, tasting me. I shiver, my hands sliding into his hair, holding him against me. But he's not trying to get away. He's staying close, slowly undoing the remaining buttons on my shirt, parting the material, tugging it free from my pants.

He pushes it off my shoulders, drags it down my arms, lets it drop to the floor.

"Fuck, Red." It's another rasp, one that has heat blooming in my stomach.

Because the way he's looking at me, the desire in his eyes, the reverent way he traces his fingers over my collar bones, down between my breasts, along my belly, gripping my hips... it's intoxicating. "Come here, baby," he orders.

"I'm already here," I whisper.

He tugs me closer, until our fronts are pressed flush together. "*Here*," he says again.

"I—"

A bend and then I'm suddenly in his arms.

He turns and settles me on the mattress. "Christ, you look good there."

Heat rolls like a wave through me and my legs press together, trying to ease the ache between them. Something he notices if his wicked grin is any indication. He drops a big palm to my thigh, spreading them wide. "Not yet, Red," he murmurs, leaning over me, kneeling between my legs.

I've imagined him coming over the top of me a hundred times, a thousand, *more* over the last couple of years.

But this is even better than all of those fantasies.

He's even better as he snakes a hand beneath me and unclasps my bra, as he kisses me deeply while palming my breasts. Then he's licking his way along my jaw, down my throat...*lower*.

"Oh, God!" I cry as he sucks one of my nipples deep, rolling the other between thumb and forefinger.

"Okay?" he murmurs against me.

"Don't stop!" I arch up into him.

"Better than okay," he teases, but thankfully, he stops talking and goes back to my nipple, drawing on it, sending pleasure cascading through me, wave after glorious wave. He kisses his way to my other breast, lavishing it with attention.

And it's like he said, slow and steady and unhurried.

Kissing his way along my belly, flicking open the button on my slacks.

My zipper goes down...then my pants, bunching around my ankles. I kick them to the side but I barely finish before his mouth is working again, this time pressing a line of kisses along the waistband of my underwear. Then drawing the fabric down. One inch and then another and then another and then—

"*Damon!*"

He grins wickedly but then repeats what sent a bolt of desire through me—dragging the flat of his tongue along my labia, lapping up the slickness of my need, holding my eyes as he repeats the action.

No hurry.

No rush.

And as each second passes, my pleasure grows. As though he's wringing out every bit of bliss from my body as he can. As though he's committing every moment to memory.

And I guess I am too.

The rough glide of his fingertips sliding over my flesh, the soft press of his lips, the light pressure of his teeth.

And all of it is good.

Is great.

Is fucking *incredible.*

And then it gets even more incredible.

Because *then* my orgasm is rolling through me.

Not in a rush or in a tsunami of sensation threatening to drag me under.

But almost gentle, as though I'm dipping my toes into the surf and it's slowly washing up and over me.

And when I come down, it's to see him kneeling between my legs, smirking like he's just flown to the moon and back.

Or maybe *I* have.

Because that orgasm...

Holy hell.

"If I didn't feel so good right now," I say lazily, "I'd kick your ass for that smile."

His grin widens.

Then he asks,

"Want me to make you smile again?"

TWENTY

Damon

NOW *SHE'S* the one who's smiling.

"You up to the challenge, hot shot?" she murmurs.

All the blood in my body—or what little is left—rushes straight for my cock.

I'm up to flying to the fucking moon and back, if she only asks.

Thankfully, in this case, the only thing she requires of me is for me to, "Get naked."

I don't even realize I'm moving before I'm on my feet and undressing. I love that her eyes are fucking greedy as hell as I tug off my shirt, greedier still when I reach for the button on my pants.

"This okay?" I ask before I undo it.

Because I have to.

Because I haven't seen any hint of fear but...

I have to make sure.

She sits up, emerald eyes warm, as though sensing my inner

battle, and then she extends her hand. "Come here," she whispers.

There's no way I can resist that.

No way I can resist anything when it comes to Joey.

I take her hand, but instead of climbing over her again, I roll to my back, bringing her over the top of me.

"Now that's a fucking sight, Red," I murmur, loving the way her cheeks go pink, the way her eyes heat again. Loving more when she bends over me and presses her mouth to mine. Tits against my chest, nails biting into my skin, thighs parted over my hips. She reaches for the button on my pants, flicks it open, and drags the material down to my hips.

My cock springs free and—

"*Fuck,*" I growl as her hand wraps around me and pumps.

Suddenly, going slow is the last thing on my mind.

"Do you have a condom?" she asks.

Christ.

But I manage—just barely—to force out past my spinning thoughts, past the urge to reverse our positions and thrust deep again and again and *again*, "Slow, baby."

"Condom," is her only reply.

Fucking *Christ*.

"In my pants," I rasp out.

She reaches behind me, yanks out my wallet.

And then I hear the glorious sound of a condom wrapper crinkling.

"Red," I groan as her fingers slowly roll the condom down my dick. Sweat breaks out on my forehead and my hands shake before I settle them on her hips and cajole, "Climb on."

Her mouth twitches. "Time for me to make *you* smile?"

Before I can reply—or maybe taste that sexy little smirk—she's sliding up my body and then...she's lowering down on top of me.

The tight clasp of her body nearly undoes me.

But not as much as her moan as she bottoms out, taking me deep. "Damon," she murmurs. "Sweetheart, you feel so good."

I can only groan in reply.

Good doesn't begin to describe it.

Every cell in my body has realigned to become in perfect sync with hers as she lifts up and grinds back down. It's better than *anything* I've ever felt.

And I know it's going to be over faster than I want.

Because already my orgasm is building, gathering at the base of my spine, ready to explode.

But I need her to get there first.

Need to watch her come apart again.

Need to—

Her nails press into my chest, her hips jerk, her pussy flutters around my cock...

Close.

She's close.

Thank fuck.

I clamp my hands onto her hips, thrusting up as she grinds down, bringing myself dangerously close to the edge, but doing it know that she's there, that she's right *fucking* there.

"Damon—" Her head drops back, her hips jerk, her mouth falls open...and her moan is the stuff of fantasies.

Then I feel it—the way she clenches around my dick, her rhythm faltering.

I keep going.

Because she's coming apart.

Because I'm so close to the edge I can't stop.

Because her pussy is far too tempting to resist.

One thrust. Another. Three more.

That's all it takes until my strokes go wild and I'm coming inside that tight cunt.

"Fuck, baby," I groan, pleasure exploding through me. My vision hazes, going black around the edges, stars flashing behind my eyes.

She collapses on top of me, but I barely feel the weight of her.

Not when I can hardly think, hardly do anything but try to exist in the aftermath of an orgasm that's nearly shredded me into a million pieces.

Eventually, my breathing settles and I manage to lift a hand, to brush back her hair and get a good look at her eyes when she lifts her head. "You doing okay?" I ask, heart suddenly in my throat. Was it too much? Did I hurt her? Remind her—

Her smile might be the best thing I've ever seen...aside from her tits, that is.

She nods.

"Kind of need the words, Red," I say, even though relief is rippling through me.

Her expression softens and she pushes up on my chest, reaching one hand up and cupping my jaw. "I'm doing pretty fucking fantastic, sweetheart."

A pulse in my chest.

In my heart.

Terrifying and exhilarating.

But mostly the second because I just had an orgasm that threatened to tear me apart, but I'm still here, whole and satisfied and with a gorgeous, sexy, *naked* woman on top of me, her pussy still clamped tightly around my dick, as though she doesn't want to let me go.

In *any* way.

I concur.

Which is why I hold her until I soften and lose that tight clasp.

I leave the bed only so long as to take care of the condom, help her drag on a tee, and put on a pair of shorts.

She's drowsy, half asleep by the time I crawl back into bed and take her in my arms.

And I'm not far behind her, my eyes sliding closed almost the moment my head hits the pillow.

But even as I drift off, I do it smiling.

UNFORTUNATELY, my smile fades about a minute after I wake up.

Because the bed is empty.

Her bag is gone.

And the T-shirt I helped her into just hours before is folded neatly and placed at the end of the bed.

Fucking hell.

TWENTY-ONE

Joey

I KNOW the guys are giving me sideways glances at practice this morning.

Not because I'm on their asses.

But because I'm smiling.

Not that I'm a hard ass normally. My coaching style is strict but fair. I don't let the guys pull one over on me (unless it's in the service of team camaraderie, like when they thought it was funny to replace all my pens with crayons and I went with drawing up the practice plans on a giant pad of construction paper). But I'm not screaming at them when a game goes to shit.

I've felt that. I hate it.

I grew up with too much yelling and I know it doesn't help these guys play better.

They know what they're doing.

They're professionals—despite the pranks and sheets of construction paper with crayon scribbles—they need a guiding hand, not someone to control every single thought and movement.

Stifle all creativity and the team loses something valuable.

Spontaneity.

And some of the best things on the ice come from giving the guys the time and space to be able to react off-the-cuff.

Today, though, all the sideways looks are making me want to have them skate lines, just so they'll stop staring at me like I'm a bug beneath a microscope. Still, I don't acknowledge the extra attention. I know if I give them any opening, I'll be giving them a mile, and they'll be all up in my business.

So, amongst the ignoring of their double takes, I do what I always do: study their movement patterns on the ice, look out for anything that seems off—players who are favoring an injury, personalities that are clashing, someone who's looking tired, chemistry or banter between guys that I haven't noticed prior to today.

This isn't a hard skate by any means.

But it is a good touch point.

My check-in done (and my smile still in place), I leave the guys to their free time.

Some will get off soon, others will stay to the end of the session.

Then it will be their chance to fuel up with protein and fast-acting carbs, take a nap, pack up their shit (because we're heading to a new city tonight after the game), and come back tonight ready to play some fucking hockey.

I'll be doing something similar, though with less napping and more prepping for this evening's game—along with the upcoming matchups on our docket.

Though, I *will* find a good restaurant to hole up at so I can eat some fast-acting carbs.

I'm thinking a huge stack of pancakes smothered with syrup. I didn't get to enjoy my last batch.

Maybe I'll see if Damon wants to eat them with me...and then smother *me* with syrup.

Perfect.

I'm thinking about that fun little epilogue to consuming delicious carbs so intently that I don't see the man standing in the hallway.

One second, I'm striding toward the conference room that I'm using as my office and the next, my arm is in an iron grip and I'm being dragged forward.

Into that conference room.

My temper spikes—I'm getting really fucking tired of him hauling me around—and I yank at my arm, trying to free it from Damon's hold.

But he doesn't release me, just slams the door shut and leans back against it. "What the fuck, Red?"

I ignore the shiver that slides through me.

I like it when he calls me Red.

Though not as much as I like him calling me baby.

I don't let that soften me.

Because, first, I was walking into this room anyway. Second, like I said, I'm tired of this man hauling me around—or well, tired of him dragging me through halls and shoving me through doors.

Third, I don't appreciate the scowl or the snapped-out question.

"What crawled up your ass this morning?" I grit.

His scowl deepens. "You're seriously going to try that shit?"

"By *shit*, you mean doing my job and then getting ready to eat something?" I cross my arms and glare at him. "I was going to invite you to get pancakes with me, you grouchy jerk. And they're really freaking good pancakes."

He doesn't seem to let that penetrate because his expression grows even more fierce. "You're the one who left this morning, *baby*." He pushes off the door, bending so his face is in mine. His hair is damp, his blue eyes spark with anger, and the scent of his cologne wraps around me.

It's almost enough to distract me.

Thankfully, I'm used to resisting all of the temptation of Damon.

I shove the thread of desire down, the same one that wrapped around me when I woke this morning, telling me to roll into Damon's sleeping form and wake him with my hands and mouth.

But we were up late last night.

He doesn't get enough sleep as it is.

So, I quietly dressed and left his room and got ready for morning skate.

That was all.

Now he's here, acting like this and—

"No pancakes for you," I growl, spinning away from him and moving over to the table, starting to pack up my shit. I need medicinal carbs. Immediately.

I ignore the silence that grows as I stuff everything into my backpack—laptop, tablet, papers, water bottle. But I can't ignore it for long.

Because my temper gets the better of me.

I zip up my backpack, lift my gaze to his, glaring at him. "And for the record, you were sleeping and I had to come to the rink. You didn't need to be here, so I let you rest."

His face changes, the asshole bleeding away.

Too late.

I'm fully pissed now.

"I thought we got somewhere last night. I—" I press my lips together then exhale. "I took a chance last night and..." I sigh.

"You're just going to be like this? I don't need another asshole in my life who's trying to control me. If I want to leave, I get to leave. If I want it to be one night, it'll be one fucking night. If I want it to be over, it'll be—"

Suddenly, he's there.

In my face, those eyes furious now.

Well, join the freaking party.

"Fuck that."

I blink. "Excuse me?" It's a dangerous question. A danger he doesn't heed.

"It's not over," he snaps. "It's not one fucking night. And you don't get to give me what you gave me, including what you gave me last night and just take it all away."

"No," I snap. "Like I said, I don't need another asshole trying to control my life."

"Red—"

"I was trying to be nice." I jab a finger into his chest. "I was trying to let you rest." Another jab. "And you know what?" I grind out. "Yes, I was going to invite you to pancakes because I know a really good place nearby, but also because I wanted a repeat of last night but with a side of freaking syrup, and you—"

But I don't get a chance to finish my insult.

Because I'm suddenly wrapped tight in his arms, his face is in mine, and he says,

"Syrup?"

TWENTY-TWO

Damon

RIGHT.

So I'm starting to think it's likely that I may have miscalculated.

But now my brain is stuck on... "Syrup?"

The barest tinge of pink appears on her cheeks but her eyes are still furious.

"Oh, fuck off," she mutters. "Now you're thinking with your dick because I hinted at sex. No"—she pushes at my chest —"this was clearly a mistake. I shouldn't have gone there and—"

I'm fucking this up.

Muddling my way through it, letting my temper take hold like usual and allowing it to fuck everything up in the process.

So...I do the only thing I can in this moment.

I kiss her.

She stills for a moment. Then her hands push at my chest

again, harder this time. I ignore her, trace my tongue over the seam of her lips and—

She softens, mouth parting, allowing me in.

Thank God.

One small thing I'm not fucking up.

But it's only when she melts against me that I lift my head.

"Damon—"

I touch her cheek. "I assumed wrong and I was a jackass, Red."

She blinks. "What?"

"Like I said, I assumed wrong. I thought you left because you regretted what happened or because I'd—" I clench my teeth together.

Her expression gentles. "You didn't do anything I didn't want, sweetheart."

That hits me hard in the chest—the endearment, the *relief*.

Thank fuck.

"Still, I get it. I fucked up, Red." I lightly trace the plump curves of her mouth. "I overreacted and I'm sorry."

Her face goes soft. "Just like that?"

"Just like what?"

"An apology," she says. "Without me having to tear it out of you?"

"Baby, I fucked up. Whenever have I doubled down on that?"

"The Berchard trade?" she says without delay, says so quickly that I can't help but laugh.

"Yeah," I admit. "I was probably wrong about letting him go, but it brought Storm to the team, so I think I win."

Her lips press together, her eyes sliding away—which tells me enough.

I've won this round.

I drop my arms, reach over, and snag her backpack.

"Wh—"

"Pancake time, Red."

"I—"

I turn the handle, flick my gaze over my shoulder at her, gaze trailing up and down that gorgeous body. "And after that... syrup."

"Uh...Coach?"

We pause our discussion of lines for tonight and I turn back to see Storm standing in the hall.

I look from Storm to Joey, not missing the longing in the kid's eyes.

I know how that feels.

But I can't deny that I have to shove down the urge to make my claim clear and public.

Not the time.

Not the place.

So, I just step a few feet away and let them have their conversation.

Though, I do it wanting to murder the kid.

Or maybe arrange another trade.

Get him the fuck out of here and far, far away from my woman.

"Damon, hey."

I snap out of my planned trade—or murder—and turn my focus to the man who's come up to me. "Yeah? Hey, Ted"—he's one of the members of the team's player development program —"what can I do for you?"

"The scouting reports you asked for are in your inbox. But I wanted to show you this." He holds up a tablet. "Personally."

There's excitement in his eyes and it takes me approximately two seconds to see why.

The kid he's showing me—the one he first identified a year ago—has gone from good to...*fucking great.*

I whistle softly.

"What is it?" Joey asks, coming close again.

But she doesn't avoid bumping into my body like she usually does. Instead, as she comes close, her tit brushes against my arm as she leans in and taps at the tablet's screen, replaying the video.

I feel her jerk and my dick likes what it does to her breast against my arm.

But I like her smile even more.

"He's good," she says.

"*Really* good," Ted agrees.

Her eyes flick to mine then turn back to Ted. "Let's bring him in."

"On it," he says and starts to hurry off.

"This is good," she murmurs.

"Yup." I lean in, drop my voice. "But it's not going to be as good as pancakes were."

Heat in her eyes as her body presses the tiniest bit closer, her breast soft and plump against me, her scent in my nose. "I thought we might have *syrup* first."

"Fuck, baby," I groan as I pump into her. "You feel so fucking good."

She arches against me, head pressing into the pillows, legs wrapped tightly around me. "No, *you* feel good, sweetheart."

A pulse in my chest.

But I'm getting used to that, used to the feel of her, used to how fucking great this feels between us.

"Oh, God!" she cries. "Right there. Don't stop. Right—" She shudders around me, pussy clamping down hard on my dick, convulsing as she comes apart.

I'm right behind her, one more stroke, two, and—

"*Fuck!*" I growl.

It should be scary how good this is, how intense my orgasm is, how hard I come with her wrapped so tightly around me, but I'm not feeling fear, not right now.

I'm not feeling much of anything except relaxed as fuck... and like I want to fuck her all over again.

"We forgot the syrup," she says lazily, trailing a foot lightly along my side.

I grin and roll over to face her, drawing her against me.

She wasn't wrong about the pancakes—they were fucking delicious—but she's right, I got so distracted that the side of syrup I brought back with us is sitting unused on the nightstand.

"Another time." It's still early.

But it's also paired with a squirm of her hips and suddenly I'm not thinking about another time.

I'm thinking about *this* time.

Rolling, I snag the container of syrup...and then I roll back and—

"Whoops."

She jumps, muscles flexing against the drop of syrup I've trailed over her belly.

"Damon," she whispers.

I bend, drag my tongue through the sticky mess.

"Syrup," I say. "*This* time."

TWENTY-THREE

Joey

"NO!" I shout. "Not a fucking chance!"

Yeah, I don't yell at my players.

The refs on the other hand...

Tonight they're going to fucking get it.

Missing two blatant penalties and an offsides that led to a goal against us (though, thankfully, my video coach was on point and advised that I use my coach's challenge, so I was able to get the goal called back). Worse, though, my guys are getting hammered and the calls are one-sided and...

We're all frustrated.

Hence my shouting.

And cursing.

"That is completely unacceptable!" I'm still shouting, trying to get the ref's attention even though the fucker seems to be purposefully ignoring me in lieu of sprinkling his focus on the other bench.

I step forward, one foot on the boards, leaning over and glaring at him. "This is bullshit and you fucking know it!"

He just...skates on by.

Fucking asshole.

I step back, teeth grinding together so fiercely that a bolt of pain shoots through my jaw. I take a breath, know that I need to find my control, that losing my temper isn't going to help anything and it sure as shit isn't going to get the assholes in black and white stripes on the ice to change their minds.

Plus, me yelling at the assholes is already going to end up on TikTok.

Last thing I need is to give the bloggers even more ammunition against me.

Kind of like sleeping with the GM?

That sends a bucket of cold water through my consciousness and I freeze.

"What do you want to do?" Tommy asks.

A breath. Two. Then I step back and mutter, "You all keep your heads. I've lost mine enough for the rest of us." One more breath and then I lift my voice. "No retaliating," I tell the guys. "No letting them get us off our plan. Let's keep grinding and focus on winning this period, yeah?"

I get a lot of nods.

A couple of amused looks.

And then Lake says, "Let's fucking go, guys, yeah?"

More nods.

Storm glances over his shoulder at me, eyes concerned.

"Focus, bud, yeah?" I say softly.

He's young but I don't miss the way my words hit him. Because I spent years feeling the same impact of Damon's words—wanting something I can't have.

Storm is a good kid.

But he's a kid.

He's too young for me, even if I was open to exploring something somehow even messier than the fire I'm playing with that's Damon and me.

And there's the power dynamic.

Messy between Damon and me.

A freaking kiss of death between me and a player.

But more than that...he's a kid.

He has an innocence that means that even in an alternate reality, he wouldn't be for me. He hasn't approached the blurry line in morality, those shadows and darkness that cling to me. He's a good kid from a good family who's got a big heart.

Not for me.

Because he wouldn't ever be able to comprehend every-thing inside me.

Unlike Damon.

Who's seen the dark underbelly of life and crawled his way out.

Who's now seen *me*.

Still stupid. Still messy. Still likely to blow up in my face.

But it's also something I can't let go of, not without seeing it through to the end.

"Yeah, Coach," he says quietly, and I hate that his eyes are a little sad before he turns and points his gaze back out to the ice.

He's young.

But he's a professional.

And he doesn't let that sadness—that I can't give him what he needs—affect his game. He jumps over the boards when it's his turn, skates hard on his shifts, and focuses on the team's game plan.

And I'm a professional too.

I ignore the blatant unfairness—though, I'm happy to report that my outburst seems to have cut out some of the most egregious calls. Things are still leaning heavily toward the other team, but we've dug out of worse holes before.

I sink back into cool and collected, work with Tommy and Dave and Kaitlyn, and by the time we go into second intermission, we're only down one goal.

Thank God.

My speech between periods is short and to the point.

"Heads down. Keep working. We've got this."

And then I leave, let Lake and company get the guys to focus.

After some extensive changes in the off-season, we've been left with a great core of players. There are still a couple guys from the old guard who are lazy and unmotivated, who don't completely buy into my choices as coach—or me as a coach at all.

But they're in the minority.

Most are good. Most can rise to the occasion that a game like tonight presents.

And most of them do.

Twelve minutes into the third, Colt Madden, one of last season's additions, picks up a great pass from Storm and drives hard into the offensive zone, dancing around their defensemen like they're cones and not living, breathing hockey players.

Colt is *fast* and has great hands.

He struggles with battles in front of the net and occasionally on the boards, but we're working on his strength there—well, he and Ivy are working on it—and Kaitlyn has suggested some adjustments to his positioning that have given him a new lease on life in those instances.

Something he proves tonight, using those great hands to make a pass to Lake before sprinting to the goal and circling tight.

Screening the goalie for just a moment.

Not getting tied up into a battle for position and taking away productive space for our guys to use.

Because he's sliding back, ceding that lane to Lake...

And then putting himself in the perfect position to receive a pass back.

Lake dekes, throws the puck, and—

I hold my breath.

Crack!

Colt's one-timer sails into the top corner of the net.

And five minutes later he, Lake, and Storm connect on another goal.

Fuck yeah.

Then it's a matter of hanging on—something made more difficult when we receive another penalty with a minute left in the game.

It's a scramble of clears and hard forechecks, solid defense and great saves by our goalie.

But we squeak it out for those two points and a satisfying as shit victory when the odds were stacked against us.

During my post-game interviews, I talk about perseverance and grinding out wins, about blatant unfairness and...I address misogynistic questions head on for a change instead of just ignoring them—

"Do you really think that it was necessary to scream obscenities at the refs?"

I *want* to scream obscenities at the smug fuck with the tape recorder pointed in my direction.

"You again," I mutter under my breath. It's the same asshole who asked about my love life.

Yup. I definitely want to invoke those obscenities.

But I find my calm, fix him in place with a stern stare, and say, "You wouldn't ask a male coach that. I'm protecting my players and sometimes that gets messy, and I will call out unfair treatment whenever necessary." A beat as I stare him down, and *fuck* it feels great when I add, "Including when it comes to me."

I allow my mouth to curve up then turn back to the rest of the reporters.

"Any other questions?"

TWENTY-FOUR

Damon

I'M STANDING in the shadows, fighting a smile.

Amused by the confident way she shut down that asshole reporter with a smug smile I want to punch off his face.

A face that I recognize from somewhere, though I don't know where.

I make a mental note to find out—mostly, so I can make sure the fucker's press credentials are revoked.

Take that, asswipe. Joey embarrasses him on camera, and then I'll take out the trash.

But aside from garbage reporters, I'm enjoying the show.

Because I'm fucking proud of her.

I sat in the box, watching the shit go down on the ice, wanting to rush down to rink level, to tear into the refs myself.

Joey had done that so I didn't have to.

Same as Joey having the asshole interviewer by the balls.

No. Having *all* of them by the balls.

I know it by her tart response, by the questions that follow —far less adversarial than before.

I know it by the way she ends the interview on her terms.

Thatta girl.

Turning, I start for the room she's using for an office.

Storm is standing outside it, still in his skates and the bottom half of his gear.

"You good?" I ask as I approach.

His eyes slide to the side, searching the hall behind me and his expression falls, I presume because he doesn't immediately spot Joey.

Damn.

The kid is going to be a problem.

"Just need to talk to Coach for a—"

His gaze jerks behind me again, and I watch his eyes light up before I turn to see Joey walking our way.

Yup.

Fuck.

The kid is *seriously* going to be a problem.

Joey's eyes drift to mine then over to Storm. A moment later she glances back to me, asks softly, "We'll talk on the plane?"

I nod. "My stuff will hold."

"Thanks," she murmurs, squeezing my forearm as she moves by me, "Storm. You need to chat?"

"Yeah, Coach. Thanks."

She pats his shoulder, tilts her head to the door.

He extends his hand, silently telling her to precede him, and though he's not a fucking pig about it, Storm looks.

At her ass.

At *my* ass.

My ass. *Mine.* Every inch of Joey is fucking mine.

Red hazes into the edges of my vision and I take a step

forward before I catch myself, my temper slipping enough to send a bucket of cold reality over my head.

Fuck.

Because it takes everything in me to stop, to not get in the kid's face, to not warn him to leave my fucking woman alone, and it takes even more to turn and walk away.

But I manage to do it, gritting my teeth together, fisting my hands, holding myself so goddamned taut that I barely breathe as I turn the corner and stride into one of the empty offices, closing the door.

Each movement careful.

Slowed.

Controlled.

So as not send a single spark toward my already primed and explosive temper.

I did that once.

And it ruined everything.

It was worth it, worth the peace it brought to my sister...but it brought a fuck-ton of pain first.

And I won't risk Joey's future.

"Fuck," I whisper, dropping my head to the door and breathing slowly.

In and out.

In and out.

This is why I don't do relationships.

This is why I keep my distance from any woman who might have a hold on me.

It's dangerous for them. And I've already proven that I can't be trusted to protect the women I care for—

Mid-spiral, my phone rings.

And I'm so fucking close to the edge that normally I would ignore it.

But it's on vibrate.

It doesn't ring for anyone other than—

"Kylie," I say after swiping across the screen and quickly lifting my phone to my ear. "Is everything okay?"

"Christ," she says on an aggrieved sigh. "I knew you'd be like this."

My eyebrows drag together. "What the hell are you talking about?"

"You care about her and you're losing it."

"About who?"

And, fuck, but that sounds exactly like the lie it is, even to my own ears.

"Nice try, big bro," she says. "Now save us both some time and lay off the excuses. Just tell me why you're freaking out about Joey."

"I'm fine."

Another lie.

And she doesn't buy this one either.

"Bullshit."

"Ky," I say. "It's getting late. I have to get ready to meet the plane."

"You do. But the game's only been over for thirty minutes. Half the guys aren't even showered yet, so there's no way anyone is waiting for you."

It's annoying how much my sister knows about my life—including how much she knows about my job.

I scowl then push off the door, rubbing the ache in my temple.

But I don't reply.

I don't need to.

She's still going.

"You and Joey," she presses. "I was at brunch, honey. I saw the sparks, and Beth agrees with me. You two..." She whistles. "The heated looks. The way your bodies orbit around each other. How you're always keeping track of exactly where she is—"

My lungs inflate on a rush of air.

But my sister's words don't stop.

"I know I told you to fix it for her and I honestly thought it would be like what you did for Ivy, for me, but Damon...there's more between you two." A beat. "And just swooping in to make things right and backing off is never going to be enough for you —not for *either* one of you."

She's not wrong.

The intractable draw. The unquenchable need.

The desire to claim and ravish and *keep*.

"And because of that—and the likelihood of alone time near horizontal surfaces by having your choice of hotel rooms—" She laughs lightly. "I'm guessing things changed for the better." My sister's voice gentles. "Even if you don't believe that right now."

Still not wrong.

Dammit, why does she have to be so fucking smart?

Why does she have to know me so well?

"You're scared, Damon."

"I can't let this happen, Ky. I *can't*. One of the players looked at her butt tonight, and I almost rammed my fist down his throat. It took everything in me to walk away. If someone does more than look, if I see Hiller—"

I clench my fists so tightly that my nails bite into my palms.

"I can't lose control like that again," I say softly. "You know why. You lived the nightmare—"

"You're not that man anymore, Damon," she replies, just as softly. "You took the classes, got the therapy. You have techniques to control your anger, and you're older and wiser and infinitely more mature. You're not going to act without thinking, not going to do something that might hurt her."

"How can you possibly believe that?"

"Because what you think was a nightmare for me—the attention, the fallout afterward—was the complete opposite."

"You hated it," I whisper.

"I hated it—*hate* it—but only because you suffered." She exhales and it's the slightest bit shaky. "Never be in any doubt that I know exactly how precious a gift it was that you gave me."

"Ky." Fuck, my eyes burn.

"Honey, you made it so I could dream again—and not just while I'm sleeping."

My throat goes tight. "*Ky*," I rasp again.

"You deserve to be more than just a man who fixes things. You deserve to have someone who looks at you the way Joey looks at you."

Heart pounding, I ask, "How does she look at me?"

There's a blip of quiet.

"You already know the answer to that, big bro. But"—her voice is gentle but laced with teasing—"since I know you're reeling, I'll give you that one."

I inhale silently, brace for the painful pleasure of the words to come.

"Like the sun rises and sets by you."

I close my eyes.

"Which, for the record, is the same way that you look at her."

TWENTY-FIVE

Joey

I CLOSE the door behind me then move to the table and lean back against the edge, not loving the look on Storm's face. "Everything okay?" I ask softly.

His lips press flat then he nods, exhales. "I'm good. I just wanted to make sure you were after that crap the refs pulled tonight."

That takes me aback for a minute.

Because *he's* worried about *me?*

"Um..." I begin.

And there I falter.

Because what the fuck?

"I just—" His eyes slide to mine and then away, and the sinking feeling in my stomach grows as the pieces click into place. Damn.

I knew this was coming.

I just...

Hoped if I kept ignoring it, kept a careful distance between us...it would just go away.

Because that worked so well between Damon and me?

I resist the urge to rub at the throb in my temple and stand still, waiting for him to finish.

Bracing for him to finish.

"Well," he says, fidgeting with the tie on his hockey pants. "I just wanted to check on you. Make sure you're good."

My fingers clench on the table's edge, hard enough to cramp, and I try to be gentle when I say, "I appreciate the sentiment, Storm, but it's not your job to check on me."

His brows pull together, hurt rippling across his face. "We're supposed to be a family, aren't we?"

A dysfunctional, incestual one clearly—no matter how hard I've been trying to fix it.

"Yes," I agree. "And like I said, I appreciate the check in, but you should be focusing on yourself and the rest of the team, not worrying about me."

His throat works, gaze coming to mine before sliding away. "It's just...Mitch"—the ref whose shenanigans were the worst tonight—"was a dick and I've never seen you that upset—"

I go for light, pointing at my hair. "I *am* a redhead." My lips twitch. "I do have a temper."

He grins. "Well, while it was the first time I've seen it, I'm seriously impressed by your use of the f word."

"Considering some of the stuff I've heard out of your guys' mouths, that's a serious compliment."

He chuckles.

I smile.

And then silence falls between us again.

I'm scrambling for a way to bring this conversation to an end, one that won't make things between us uncomfortable and awkward for the foreseeable future, while at the same time racking my brain to start erecting some professional barriers, but—

I don't get that far.

Because he steps a little closer, eyes sliding to mine and away again. "Coach..." A shake of his head. "I mean, Joey—"

Shit.

"I know this is unconventional and probably crosses more than a few lines, but—" He moves closer, takes his hand in mine, squeezing lightly. "I was wondering if you might like to go out to dinner sometime."

Fuck.

I pull my hand free, slip free, and step to the side—

His face.

Fucking hell. His beautiful, innocent *face.*

"Storm," I say quietly. "I can't. I..." I take a breath because again, I don't want to hurt him and I need to be measured and controlled in my response. But...this cannot be.

Not ever.

"Look," I tell him. "You're a good kid—"

He flinches.

"A good man," I correct, trying to go gently, but knowing there's no way to actually make this better. "But even putting aside the fact that I'm your coach and you're my player, I...I don't feel the same way about you as I think you do about me."

He's quiet for a long moment.

Long enough that I'm dying a slow death inside, inch by painful inch.

"Fuck," he mutters, shoving a hand through his hair. "*Fuck.* I'm sorry," he rasps. "I shouldn't have—" He clamps his mouth together. "Forget I said anything, I—"

He turns away, chin dropping to his chest, not speaking for long enough that my skin starts aching and I'm desperate to get the hell out of here.

But he's between me and the door and...

He needs time to process this isn't what he hoped it was in his head and heart.

That it can't *ever* be.

So, I wait in silence, give him that quiet, that time...since I can't give him what he wants.

Eventually, he turns and looks up at me, his expression drawn, his eyes sad. "Just forget I said anything, okay?"

I nod, reply softly, "Okay."

A jerk of his chin before he starts for the door.

Then he stops again, turns back, his eyes connecting with mine over his shoulder, and drops a bomb on me.

"It's because of Damon, isn't it?"

I SIGH as I sink onto the bed, completely exhausted.

And yet, I'm wired, ready to take on the world—or at least ready to create my plan for the game the following night.

The plane ride was a short one, the mood quiet with most of the guys getting a quick nap in before touchdown—the single members of the team needing their energy to go out and tie one on, taking advantage of the free day tomorrow by staying up late and partying hard. Those in relationships usually hang closer to the hotel. They might go out for a drink or a late dinner before heading up to their rooms and calling home.

But they'll be tucked into bed snoozing well before the others make it home.

Me?

I spent the flight getting ahead of tomorrow's work.

Now I'm in my room.

Alone.

And it's hard not to think of Storm's face when he said, "*It's because of Damon, isn't it?*"

Harder still to not think of how his expression changed when he read whatever answer was in mine.

Hurt.

No, anguish.

And, fuck, but I spent several years in that same agony.

I hate that I've made him feel the same way.

So, yeah, maybe my restlessness is less to do with being ready to make my plans for tomorrow and more about...

Guilt.

Yup. I feel like an asshole.

Sighing, I push up out of bed again and reach for the menu on the bedside table. I need empty calories, preferably ones made up of simple sugars...like those I might find in a giant ice cream sundae.

With extra hot fudge and cherries.

Thank God, they have it on the menu.

A bath, a sundae, and maybe...

I'll text Damon.

Our eyes had connected on the plane, but then he'd been pulled into a conversation with the assistant GM, and Tommy had wanted to check in, and because the flight wasn't long, we hadn't shared more than that look.

But there was something in his eyes.

Something...*off*.

So bath, sundae, and maybe I'll tackle whatever that *off* means in the morning.

Because I know that's the most logical course of action, I crawl out of bed, snagging the receiver and hitting the button for room service.

It rings once, a woman coming on the other end, and just as

I'm completing my order—with a firm emphasis on extra whipped cream and cherries—there's a knock at the door.

My pulse speeds, fear and anticipation mixing.

Clashing.

Not Hiller, not ever again.

Which means...

That anticipation grows, takes over.

The knock comes again.

Along with a voice.

"Let me in, Red."

Smiling, I hang up and hurry over to the door.

TWENTY-SIX

Damon

THE PIZZA IS BURNING the shit out of my arm, but I'm precariously holding on to the six-pack of beer so I can't shift it, even to save myself from the third degree burns.

Yes, I'm being dramatic.

Also, yes, the pizza is fucking *hot*.

I knock again, the beer bottles rattling in the cardboard holder, calling, "Let me in, Red."

Not loudly.

I don't know who's staying on this floor, and I don't want to draw extra attention to me showing up at Joey's door.

Not now.

Not when I'm barely holding on.

When we're...

New.

When we haven't figured out how we're going to deal with us being us when us being *us* is messy and complicated and—

Scary as fuck.

The door swings open.

Fuck, she's beautiful.

Still in the white button-down and slacks, feet bare, toes painted a pale pink.

"What are you—"

I step forward, thankful when she retreats, backing into the door and giving me an opening. I slip inside, hurry to the table shoved in the corner, and set the pizza and beer down. "Jesus," I mutter, shaking my arm out, soothing the overheated skin.

She giggles. "What's it with hockey boys and the dramatics?"

I narrow my eyes at her. "I bring you pizza and you just laugh at my pain?"

"Try having a period once a month and then talk to me about pain," she quips back without missing a beat.

And considering I've never had a period—and that I also hope to get laid tonight, despite the fears and complications and messiness—I don't argue, just nod at the pizza and ask, "You hungry?"

She crosses her arms, leans back against the door. "I just finished ordering food from room service."

"Liar," I tease.

Her chin lifts. "I'm not lying."

I know that. Because I know *her*. Same as I know that she didn't order *actual* food. "You called down and put in an order for a sundae."

Those eyes go wide.

My mouth hitches up. "With extra whipped cream and cherries."

Those wide eyes go wider.

"I know you, baby."

"Apparently," she says dryly. Then she narrows her eyes at me, warning, "I only ordered one."

Amusement bubbles up in my chest and I shake my head as I open the box. "I bring pizza and beer and I can't even bum a bite of hot fudge."

"I had plans for a bath and my sundae, not a hulking hockey player invading—"

"Former," I correct, thoroughly enjoying the sass she's tossing my way.

"Not a *former* hulking hockey player invading my space and trying to get his hands on my goodies," she says, not missing a beat. "Even *if* he does come bearing beer and pizza."

There's a comment there about what goodies I'm going to get my hands on, but I keep that thought in my head and tease back, "Even if said former hockey—"

"*Hulking* hockey player."

I grin, correct, "Even if said former *hulking* hockey player comes bearing your favorite beer?" I knew I was making the right choice in shoving down the fear and listening to Kylie when I saw the small brewery's ale in the cold case at the pizza joint. "*And* your favorite type of pizza?"

"Even then," she says, chin lifting.

"Ouch," I joke, clamping a hand to my chest.

But she's smiling too, and...she's walking my way. She wraps her fingers around mine, drawing both of our hands down my chest. "Maybe I'll share *one* bite." Just as we reach the good stuff—the waistband of my pants—she drops my hand, reaches around me, and snags a slice. "...of this pizza."

She tears off a huge chunk, moans as she chews, swallows. "Oh, this is good. Maybe even better than a sundae."

"Better than me licking that sundae off your naked skin and then us sharing a bath?"

She chokes, eyes going wide.

I grin, gently pat her on the back. Then open a beer and

pass it over to her, waiting until she's stopped coughing to take my own slice.

"So, that game tonight..." I say, even though I'd rather talk about getting her naked and wet.

That'll come.

Heh. She'll come.

But later. I want this time with her, need to make sure she's good.

Plus, room service delivery people always seem to have the worst timing.

She sets the beer down, folds the slice of pizza in half, and takes another bite, chewing and swallowing without the side of choking fit. "You going to chastise me for yelling at the refs?"

"Fuck no." The blatant favoritism was atrocious.

"Then are you going to ask me if I'm okay taking them on?"

"Also, fuck no," I say. "You're a tough cookie, Joey. You're not about to let a couple of asshole refs rattle you."

"That's not what Storm thinks," she mutters.

I still.

Then curse under my breath. "He told you that?"

She rubs her temple. "No." A sigh. "He wanted to make sure I was good." She groans softly. "Right before he tried to ask me out."

I curse again, but this time it's not under my breath. "Tell me that dumb fuck didn't actually ask you out?"

She nods morosely. "Yeah," she says softly. "I made it clear that couldn't happen." She drops the pizza back into the box, sits back and sighs. "But I hurt him, and God, Damon what we're doing—" Her gaze comes to mine and she shakes her head. "Is it really much better?"

"Of course it fucking is. There's no power dynamic for one—"

"Come on," she mutters. "If you really wanted to get me fired, I have no doubt you could make that happen."

Shit. "Baby—"

"For another, if the press finds out—" She drops her hands into her head.

"Here's the thing, Red." I sigh, but it's not in impatience. It's because I know that my mind hasn't been much of a better place myself, spinning around and around as I war with what's right and what I want, what I'm scared of and what we might have. "Logic says this is stupid, that we should keep our distance, stay as work acquaintances at best, friends at worst. Logic says this will likely blow up in our faces and then we'll be left cleaning up the pieces. I'm a man with a record who's spent the last decade in anger management and who could technically throw a big enough fit to have you removed from your job. You're a woman who's been through hell and back and deserves a fuck of a lot better than me. But even though logic is screaming and the facts don't line up and it would make more sense if we didn't keep going with this—"

Her lungs inflate in a rush, but I continue talking.

"Even though there are a hundred reasons why we *shouldn't* do this, all I know is that I've come to the conclusion that the only thing I *can't* do is let you go."

She lifts her head and I hold her gaze.

"The only question is if you feel the same way."

TWENTY-SEVEN

Joey

I OPEN my mouth to answer, even though I don't know what the hell I'm going to say.

What the hell *can* I say to something as wonderful as that—

And I'm interrupted by a knock at the door.

Damon goes still, eyes slicing toward the heavy panel as though he has lasers in those bright blue irises, lasers that can cut through the material and disintegrate whoever's dared to interrupt this conversation.

But—

"My sundae!" I exclaim.

His head jerks, and heat floods my cheeks.

Thankfully, he's smiling as he leans in, brushes his thumb over the pink I presume is spreading on my face. "Your sundae," he murmurs, tugging me close and pressing his lips to my forehead.

Then he stands and moves to the door, answering it, and coming back while I'm still reeling from that soft touch of his mouth. He's holding my dessert and I watch as he lifts his free hand, dips a finger into the whipped cream—my *extra* whipped cream!—and brings it to his mouth.

"That's mine!" I cry.

His mouth quirks, eyes dancing. "Is this you telling me that your extra whipped cream is more important than what we were talking about?"

Horror whips through me.

But then he comes closer and I get a good look at his face, see that he's teasing me, and my always present sass (at least with Damon) makes itself known. "Maybe not the whipped cream"—I lean in, pluck up one of the maraschino cherries—"but the cherries are *definitely* more important than what we were talking about."

I pop it into my mouth and chew, the explosion of sweetness hitting my tongue. But when I reach for the second one, he swings it out of reach.

"Damon!"

A wicked smile, but there's an edge of seriousness in his blue eyes that has me dropping my obsession with the sundae and focusing back on what's important.

Only, I don't have fancy words. I don't have anything eloquent, anything that could possibly equate to what he said before the knock at the door.

All I have is...

"I feel the same way."

The transformation in his eyes takes my breath away.

His reaction does too.

But mostly because it's freezing cold.

"Whoops," he says, upending the sundae on me.

I shriek in surprise, but it's cut off by his mouth coming down on mine, the remnants of the sundae squished between us, soaking into our clothes. His tongue slips between my parted lips, tangling with mine at the same time he starts in on my buttons.

I gasp as the sundae slops down the open front of my shirt, drips into my bra.

Then gasp again when his mouth lifts from mine and—

I moan, head dropping back as his tongue trails along my skin, lapping up the remains of— "My sundae!"

He chuckles, the heat of his breath on my flesh, tangling with the cold, making me shiver and arch against him, hold him close. "Don't worry, baby," he murmurs, tongue and lips working. "I'll order you another one."

My lungs hitch and it's not because I'm worried about the sundae, nor because I'm worried about the ice cream and hot fudge and cherries and whipped cream wasteland between us. But rather, it's the glorious things he's doing with that tongue and mouth and those lips. It's the reverent way his hands are moving on me, undoing my bra, pushing it and my shirt to the floor.

Down.

Down.

Down.

My throat. My breasts. My belly. My hips.

Down to the waistband of my pants, flicking open the button, tugging down the zipper...and they join my shirt on the floor.

His slips his fingers into my underwear, sends them sailing too.

And then I'm naked.

"Look at *my* dessert," he murmurs, trailing his fingers through the sticky mess, circling the hard bud of one nipple and then the other. "All pink"—he dips those fingers between my legs then lifts them, glistening with the evidence of my desire, to his lips and sucks deeply—"and sweet—"

I gasp.

Then he's scooping me up, tossing me on the bed.

I bounce once and then he's grabbing my ankles, yanking my hips to the edge of the bed, spreading my legs. "*Mine.*" Then his mouth is on me, doing wonderful things, doing fucking *incredible* things.

Fingers and teeth, lips and tongue.

It's like he's memorized every moment of the night before, everything I liked, everything that made me gasp and moan, everything that drove me closer to orgasm.

And he's not going slow tonight.

This is a man determined, a man exploiting that knowledge...to my very pleasurable benefit.

"Wait," I murmur as I feel my orgasm closing in, the tremors beginning, my nerves firing, my hips bucking, grinding against him. "Wait, sweetheart," I say, trying to slow myself, trying to find control. "I want to come with you."

He doesn't wait.

He also doesn't stop.

But he lifts his head, wicked grin in place. "You'll come with me"—he strokes a finger through my slick pussy—"but you're also going to come now."

Then he drops his head.

And he's right.

I come mere moments later, and I'm still feeling that pleasure ripple through me as he strips off his clothes and climbs over the top of me.

"Inside," I beg.

He doesn't delay, spreading my legs, stroking deep.

I wrap my legs around him, clenching tight as he starts fucking me hard and fast. No delay. No quarter. Just taking the edge of my orgasm and driving me up to an even higher peak.

And he's right.

I came before.

And I'm coming now. With him.

His strokes go jerky and uneven, my name tumbles off his lips, and then he collapses on top of me, both of us breathing heavy.

But it's what he says when we eventually catch our breath that has me falling a little in love with Damon Connors.

"Now *that* was a sundae."

TWENTY-EIGHT

Damon

FUCK, she's beautiful, even in the morning.

Sunshine pouring in through the windows, creating patterns on her skin I want to trace with my fingers and tongue.

But we were up late last night.

Enjoying that first sundae, chasing it with pizza and beer, then enjoying the second sundae I ordered for her just as much —even though she was the one eating it.

Of course, because she was licking it off my naked body, I wasn't complaining.

The only thing we didn't get to was the bath.

But I have plans for that...preferably the jetted one in my master bathroom after I've sent my sister away for a long weekend.

Now, though, she's out, as in *out* so I'm going to let her sleep while I get some fresh clothes and then search out some food for us.

She'll have work to do—she always does.

So food and work and then I'm going to sweep her away for something fun.

Because she hasn't had enough fun in her life.

Bending, I press my lips to her naked shoulder, smiling when she sighs and burrows into the pillows, then quietly dress in my stiff and sticky clothes.

I snag the keycard from the dresser, shove it into my pocket, and slip from the room.

Unfortunately, my focus on that slipping, on closing the door quietly so as not to wake her up means that I don't make sure the hall is clear.

And because of that—

"Hey."

I miss that one of my players, Colt, is behind me.

I jump, nearly undoing all that slipping and quiet then turn to look at the power forward.

He's studying me with shrewd brown eyes—eyes that flick down to my chest and pants—before coming back up to mine.

"Morning," I mutter.

He's silent for a beat then says, "Yeah, seems like you had a good one." He smirks. "Or a good night anyway."

Before I can comment on that, he starts off down the hall.

"Right," I say under my breath, thankful he's not going to make this anymore awkward than it already is.

Then again, I've seen the parade of women flowing in and out of his hotel room.

The other man has no room to talk.

A door slams down the hall and I shake myself.

Ass in gear.

Clean clothes. Food. Not fucking up the morning after I finally got my head straight about Joey, after she's finally admitted she wants me back.

Thankfully, there are no further hiccups as I accomplish

the first—taking a quick shower, throwing on a fresh shirt and pants.

The second part of that, though...

"You need to promise me something."

I still, mid-load-up of my two plates at the breakfast buffet, and glance over at the kid who's trying to murder me with his stare.

Considering I wanted to do the same thing to him yesterday, I clamp a lid on my temper.

"Storm," I say quietly. "Good game last night."

His expression doesn't change in the least. "I need you to promise me something."

I exhale silently, know that as much as I don't want to have this conversation here and now—let alone anywhere or *ever*—the kid clearly has something to say to me. "What do you need me to promise you?"

"You need to protect her."

I blink. "Joey?"

His eyes flash. "Yeah, fucking Joey."

"Look, kid—"

"I'm not a fucking kid," he snaps. "I'm old enough to know that what I want isn't reciprocated. I get that. I'm not exactly cool with it, but I'm not one of those fucks who takes what he wants no matter if a woman wants it or not, so I'll deal. But what I need from *you*"—he steps closer, voice dropping, threat laced through every syllable—"is for you to promise me that you'll protect her, that you'll look after her, that you'll make sure she's happy and loved and safe."

The word *loved* sends a bolt of panic through me, but I shove it down enough to focus on the rest of his words.

"Because she deserves that much and more," he says. "She deserves the world and—" He exhales sharply. "She deserves a man who can give that to her."

"Storm," I begin.

"Promise me, Damon."

I settle a hand on his shoulder, hold tight when he goes to shake me off. "I know exactly how precious a gift I have, okay?"

He opens his mouth.

"So, I'm not going to squander it or throw it away." My fingers flex. "But I can also promise you that I'll look after her. That I'll protect her and keep her safe and happy."

His nostrils flare.

I shake him lightly. "Okay?"

He nods. "Okay."

"Now, I need you to promise *me* something."

His eyes hold mine, flaring with frustration, a muscle in his jaw ticking. But to his credit, he just blows out a breath then asks quietly, "What do you need me to promise you?"

"That you'll start looking after yourself." I drop my hand. "That you'll start focusing on what you *can* have and then you'll enjoy the fuck out of it."

He's still for a long moment.

Then he blows out another breath. But I don't miss that it's paired with his lips curving up, with amusement sliding into his eyes. "I can't promise that."

I open my mouth.

"But I can promise to give it my best fucking try."

I clap him on the shoulder and grin. "That's all I can ask, kid."

A shake of his head, the anger leaving his frame—and I'm fucking glad for it. He deserves more too.

He grabs his plate and starts to turn away.

Then pauses, looks back.

"I'm never going to outgrow that, am I?"

"Being called a kid?"

He nods.

"Nah." I chuckle. "Sorry, kid. You're stuck with it forever."

A sigh.

But he's smiling as he walks away.

I am too as I finish loading up my plates then hit the elevators, eyes hitting on a brochure by the front desk that has Joey's name written all over it.

I put the plates down, snag it, scanning the description.

After I make a quick call, my smile widens even further.

Because I know this is right, this is exactly what Joey and I both need, and I'm smiling because I know that in less than two minutes I'll be pushing through the door to her room, seeing that gorgeous naked body of hers that I can touch and stroke, kiss and hold.

So fuck yeah, I'm smiling.

Because I know I'm returning to something sweeter than life itself.

TWENTY-NINE

Joey

"WHERE ARE WE GOING?" I ask as Damon tugs open the back door of the Lyft.

He doesn't answer until I've slid into the car and he's plunked into the seat next to me.

"It's a surprise."

I blink.

"But you know—"

"That you hate surprises?" He winks at me, mouth curved into a sexy smile. "Oh, yeah, Red. I know."

The car pulls away from the curb as I'm sputtering.

He leans close, lips coming to my ear. "But I promise you'll love this one."

I spin in my seat, lifting my brows before I settle my hand on his thigh, shifting near so he can hear me when I murmur, "I would have *loved* staying in my room and having a repeat of last night, considering it's our day off."

A nip to my ear. "Liar."

I shiver. "Ex-excuse me?"

"I said"—a flick of his tongue—"you're a liar."

"I'm not lying," I hiss. "I happen to like very much what we did last night."

"Oh, of that I'm not in doubt. What you're lying about is the repeat—"

"I—"

"Not because you don't mean it, Red." He brushes his nose along my jaw. "But because something would undoubtedly come up and you'd find yourself working."

I grin. "You only say that because you'd find yourself doing the same thing."

He presses his lips to my forehead. "Maybe."

"No *maybe* about it." I lean my shoulder against his. "Now, what's this surprise?"

"The surprise"—he shifts, wraps his arm around me and tugs me closer—"is that it's going to *remain* a surprise until we get there." A kiss to the top of my head. "Which, thankfully, won't take much longer."

He jerks his chin to the windows, and I frown, realizing that we've somehow left the city proper and are in the rolling hills dotted with farms that chase suburbia into the more heavily populated areas.

"Where—"

The driver exits the freeway, turning up into those rolling hills, bright green and dotted with trees, separated into plots with wooden and wire fences.

Frowning, trying to make sense of it all, I mutter, "Taking me off to be murdered then, are you?"

The driver huffs out a laugh, her eyes connecting with mine for a second in the rearview.

"Maybe she'll tell me where we're going," I half-threaten.

"And ruin the surprise?" she says. "Absolutely not."

Damon laughs and even though I'm frowning on the outside, inside I'm doing the same.

And, anyway, there's not really a surprise to ruin any longer.

Because we're turning again, this time onto a narrow track road, waist-high grass on one side, growing up to a giant sign.

A sign that ruins the surprise.

My eyes go wide and my head jerks so fast I nearly give myself whiplash as my gaze connects with Damon's. "Seriously?"

He nods, mouth curving. "Seriously."

My reply is hushed, almost reverent. "How did you—?"

He touches my cheek. "Because I know you." He leans closer, taps the tip of my nose. "And because I saw the picture in your office, Red."

"I—" My eyes burn and I hold my breath, blinking rapidly. This is too much. I can't handle this. I can't accept it. I can't—

"Breathe, Red," he murmurs, smoothing a hand up and down my arm. "I saw a brochure for this place at the hotel this morning. They happened to have space and..." A shake of his head. "It was kismet."

I release a trembling breath. "No," I whisper. "It was *you*."

His thumb brushes lightly over my cheek and I only realize he's wiping a tear away when he orders softly, "Don't cry."

"Sweetheart..."

Soft blue eyes. A gentle kiss to my forehead. A...

Sniff from the front seat.

"Sorry," the driver says as we take a right and pull into a small dirt parking lot. "It's just good to see that romance is alive and well."

"Whoever would have thought grumpy, broody Damon Connors would be a romantic at heart?" I tease lightly.

His eyes dance, but he just presses a kiss to my nose before looking forward. "Thanks for the ride," he tells our driver. "And if you want to come back in three hours, I'll pay you in cash for a lift back to our hotel."

She turns in her seat, eyes coming to mine. "I'll see you then." A wink at me. "Enjoy the romance."

Damon pops open the door, holds out a hand for me.

Then we're in the cool fall air...

And it's not ten minutes before I'm living one of my dreams.

"Moo!"

I squeal softly and lean closer, scratching the baby Highland cow—or *coo*, as our Scottish transplant guide calls them. The adorable fluff ball, my absolute favorite animal on the planet, moos again and shifts so I can get on scratching the spot he really likes—behind his ears.

And I've melted.

Or maybe I did from the moment we walked onto the farm and met our guide, hearing the story of how the farm came to be—a drunken bet and a long journey with just five cows...that have now become a herd of thirty.

We brushed the juveniles, dropped hay for the adults, posed in a 4x4 by the prettiest coo in the world (complete with the fancy fashion magazine covers to prove it), and now we're in a large barn, getting to love on a trio of baby cows, all of whom were rejected by their mothers. Which is the only thing that gave me a blip of sadness—that they weren't out there with the rest of their herd family—but not for long.

Because we got to enjoy them.

And because they'll have a nice, peaceful future with

plenty of hay and a pasture to graze on when they're old enough.

"Moo!" his bro exclaims, nudging in for some of my scratching action. And who am I to deny him his loving?

But even as I'm giving cuddles and scratches all around, I'm trying to brace myself.

Because my three hours are almost up.

Because our guide has a life and duties to get back to.

Because our ride is back in the parking lot, waiting to drive us home.

"Maybe I'll quit my job and start a farm," I say, only half-joking.

"We could keep the job and get one as a pet," Damon says, and my heart practically explodes at the gentle way he cuddles the last baby.

"I'm not sure our jobs our conducive with cow raising."

"Who are you kidding?" His lips twitch. "The guys would love a mascot on the plane."

I grin, imagining one of these goofballs mooing their way across the country, then I give them all one more scratch and straighten, committing this to memory as I say my goodbyes and then thank our guide.

Damon follows my lead, tipping our guide before we wash up and head for the car.

Before we make it that far, I take his hand, drawing him to a stop.

"You good, Red?" he asks, tucking a strand of my hair behind my ear so gently that my heart pulses.

Or maybe it's just open and raw and vulnerable and... *falling* hard and fast.

"I need you to know something," I whisper.

His eyes are serious, but he stops, nods, and waits for me to go on.

"This was the nicest thing anyone has ever done for me."

He opens his mouth, but I squeeze his fingers, cutting him off.

"And..." I find the courage to finish. "When I'm with you—coos or not—I need you to know that I don't feel empty."

His eyes flare.

"I won't forget today," I murmur. "And I won't forget *that*. And I promise you I'll find a way to make you feel everything I'm feeling right now."

Because he deserves that.

Because whether or not he realizes it, his life has been far too empty too.

He starts to shake his head. "I don't expect—"

I place my free hand over his mouth, lean in, and know that it's not really a matter of falling for him. That happened years ago. Today, these last couple of weeks...I've already *fallen*. "I know you don't expect anything in return, sweetheart." I drop my hand, lean in, and kiss him with everything I'm feeling. "And that," I murmur when I lift my head, heart pounding, "is exactly why I'm making you this promise."

"Red—"

"No more emptiness. Not for either of us."

THIRTY

Damon

I'VE BEEN on the phone all fucking day.

And I hate being on the fucking phone.

It's—hands down—the worst part of my job.

Scouting new guys, working on trades, watching games and checking out our competition, keeping my finger on the pulse of how other teams in our division—and the league as a whole—are playing...all of those are fine.

Hell, they're fun most of the time.

I can even tolerate the other shit—talking with legal, doing the limited press I do (because Joey does an excellent job of being the face and voice of the team), tracking trades and budgets and performance reviews.

But talking on the phone—especially in the early days of negotiating contracts that end this season—is hell.

Especially when one of those contracts belongs to Lake Jordan.

He's the biggest hit to our salary cap.

And he deserves the money he's pulling.

But his agent is a fucking shark, so adding insult to injury, it's not just one call. It's a string of phone calls and they're painful phone calls and they're *necessary* phone calls.

Fucking annoying as shit.

"I can make that happen," I tell her when she finishes listing out several more concessions we'll have to make— including a three-team trade clause.

Meaning, if we ever have to move him, it'll be only to one of those three teams.

See?

Fucking pain in my ass.

And he has the skills, points, and experience to make that demand.

Same as I know, he's the player who'll continue carrying the team forward...so we'll bend over backwards to give it to him.

"Good," Olivia says and I rue the day that Prestige Media Group was founded. "I'll be in touch in a few weeks once the other details are finalized."

"Great," I mutter.

"As always, Damon," she says breezily, "it's a pleasure doing business with you."

"Right." It's still a mutter and it's paired with me hanging up the phone.

Scowling, I lean back in my chair.

Then my phone rings again.

"Jesus Christ," I snap, sighing before I swipe a finger across the screen and lift my cell to my ear. "Yes?"

The person on the other end starts speaking and I barely hold back a groan.

Because this isn't going to be a short call.

"Are you there?" they ask.

I allow my head to drop back, staring up at the fluorescent lights in the ceiling, and then I get on with doing the worst part of my job—saying all the right things at the right times and resisting the urge to call the person on the other side of the phone an idiot.

In the end, I succeed.

But just barely.

I PUSH out of the office, turn in the direction of the parking lot.

If I've been punished with phone calls all morning and afternoon, at least I can do is get out of here early.

I'll grab some food, bring it over to Joey's place, and fuck out all of my frustrations.

Or maybe we'll finally get to have that bath.

It's been two weeks since the night of the sundae—or rather, *sundaes*—and aside from the copious amounts of phone calls and the watchful eye of Storm, these have been the best weeks of my life.

Easy. Full.

Joey.

Maybe that's the best adjective.

Because *she's* the one making my life easy, making me feel alive, making every minute with her better than the last.

So yeah...maybe tonight is bath night.

I have a mind to show her exactly how much I appreciate all of that.

Tomorrow is a scheduled day off. We can stay up late, I can fuck her exactly how I want, and then do the same thing in the morning before I treat her to pancakes.

Good plan.

Break.

But I don't make it to the parking lot.

Hell, I don't even make it five feet down the hall before my phone rings again.

"Fuck," I mutter, pulling it out of my pocket.

"That good, huh?" Colt says, walking by with his messenger bag hitched on one shoulder, clearly here taking advantage of the free ice time that Joey arranged for the team this afternoon.

"It's the job," I grumble. "But not a fun part of it."

"Hopefully it'll be a quick one."

I nod my thanks, turn back for the office, and answer the call.

Spoiler alert: it's *not* a short one.

But it eventually ends, and I start to leave again.

The fuck of it all is that when I'm attempting to make my escape—this time with Colt passing me, now completely geared up—my cell rings a-fucking-*gain*.

His eyes come to mine and he winces.

I just drop my chin to my chest, walk into my office, and answer, listening to an update from a scout.

The best thing is that it's short.

When it's done, I hang up and glare down at my phone. "Don't you fucking ring again." It stays silent. "That's right, asshole," I mutter.

I shove it in my pocket and...wait.

When it doesn't immediately ring again, I release a relieved breath, gather up the rest of my shit, and push out into the hall again.

There, I wait again, half expecting my phone to go off.

Because that's my day today.

When it doesn't, I turn down the hall.

Unfortunately, my escape is stymied yet again.

Not by a phone call.

But rather, by a voice.

"Damon?" I hear.

Biting back a curse, I turn to see that Colt's back a third time. He's still dressed in his gear—which means that, thank fuck, I haven't lost a year to the fucking phone calls, just a few hours.

"Yeah?" I ask him, hoping that I sound patient.

Based on the way he smiles, I have the feeling I fail at that.

Though, he doesn't seem offended. Instead, he grins as he holds up a stick and pair of skates.

"I think you may need these more than me."

THIRTY-ONE

Joey

HE DIDN'T TEXT.

Or come to my office.

And he isn't in *his* office.

Frowning, I scroll through my phone, half-expecting a text to pop up as I wander through the halls.

They're buzzing with an interesting type of energy, one I'd likely pay more attention to if I wasn't staring at my cell's screen, perplexed by the sudden disappearance of my boyfriend.

The *crack* of sticks connecting with the ice, the echoes of pucks hitting the boards, the din of male voices giving each other crap...it takes a second, but eventually, I process what I'm hearing.

Strange.

I arranged the ice time.

But the guys mostly use it to fuck around, to practice individual skills, to unwind or try out a new play.

It's generally fairly quiet, only a handful of players using it at a time.

The noise I'm hearing...

It's more than that.

Much more.

I pick up the pace without really realizing it, tucking my phone into the back pocket of my jeans as I push through the door to the practice rink.

"Oof," I mutter several moments later when the door slams into my back.

Because I've frozen in the opening, trying to process what I'm seeing in front of me.

"Damon," I whisper, shoving the door off me and stepping fully into the rink.

"I know," I hear, jumping about five feet in the air. Kylie smiles at me, her fingers finding mine and squeezing in silent apology for startling me. "I couldn't believe it when I saw it either."

She looks back out onto the ice and I do the same.

Because...he's out there.

In skates and gloves, a stick in his hand, moving gracefully as he carries a puck, stick handling fluidly, eyes up as he passes the biscuit over to Colt.

One touch brings it back to Damon who continues fucking around, bouncing the puck off one skate and forward, returning it to the blade of his stick, then firing it back to Colt. Back and forth, nothing too fancy, and there are definitely moments where I can see Damon is rusty from not having played in a long time.

But the instincts are there, the talent is being buffed to a beautiful shine, and—

Crack!

My mouth quirks.

He's still got that killer slapshot.

"Wow," I murmur.

"I know," Kylie says, leaning next to me, resting her hands on the dasher and peering through the glass. "I remember going to his games. It used to be my favorite part when he made that shot. Like he was a superhero sending the puck at super speed."

She falls quiet.

I do too.

And I know it's because she's feeling the same thing I am— mourning he lost that, mourning the cost to both her and Damon.

"He told me, you know," she whispers.

My lungs inflate on a rush of air. I hold that inhale for a moment then push it out. "I know," I say softly.

"And he promised me he would make it better for you."

My head jerks toward her. "Kylie—"

"I don't say that to take away anything he's doing for you," she murmurs, fingers squeezing mine again. "But because I noticed how you looked at him and I liked—*like*—you. You're nice and funny and smart and I knew, even with that wicked combination of temptation, he'd continue to keep his distance unless..."

"Unless?"

Her eyes gentle. "Unless I gave him a push." She leans close, bumps her shoulder against mine. "Same as I know that Beth had to make the hard sell to you."

I snort. "Beth doesn't know anything *aside* from the hard sell." I smile at her. "But she's been surprisingly chill about me and Damon. Probably because"—I grin at her—"your brother has enough stubbornness for all of us combined."

"True." She grins back. "Though, I suppose she's saving the hard sell for me, considering the twice weekly phone calls I've been getting since her visit."

I groan. "Oh no."

"Oh yes," she says. "I've heard all about how I need to get back out there and live my life—something that pains me to admit she's right about because it's far beyond time I stop hiding." A huffed-out breath. "All I'm saying is that I know your pain."

My heart twinges. "Do you need me to tell her to back off?"

Kylie smiles. "No," she says. "I miss that—having someone in my business..."

"Driving you crazy?" I supply when her eyes grow sad, knowing it's probably because she misses her mom.

A giggle, light sliding back into her face. "Yes. *That.*" She leans against the glass. "I'm glad you have her."

"You know that you have her too now?"

Her teeth press into her bottom lip. "Yeah?"

"Yup. If Beth and John have nothing else, it's sticking power."

"Like a fungus?"

"More like funk to a hockey glove," I say solemnly.

She giggles again then nods out onto the ice. "You ever miss it?"

"Sometimes," I say. "There's nothing better than the slight sting in your palms when a puck lands on your blade or the high you get connecting a great pass. Scoring is great," I say. "But I swear, there was nothing better than setting someone else up and seeing their face light up when they buried it in the back of the net." I shake my head and laugh. "Which is probably why I ended up coaching when my knee couldn't hack it— I got to make the plays and be in control and still get the high of a great play, a great goal, a great pass, a great game."

Her mouth quirks. "I feel that same high when I manage to binge a trash reality show while crocheting a perfect line of stitches."

Blinking, not expecting that in the least, I turn to her. "Explain."

Her cheeks go a little pink. "And the Head Coach Voice comes out." But before I can apologize for what she's correct about—my demanding tone—she laughs and says, "There's nothing to talk about. In that vein of trying to live my life, I'm learning something new."

"Crocheting?"

She nods. "And because I'm terrible at it, I'm pairing it with something I like."

"Trashy reality shows?"

Another nod. "And wine."

"Which is your favorite?"

"Wine or show?"

She smiles as she names her favorite wine and then *I'm* smiling when she mentions a trashy reality show that I happen to watch with religious accuracy. "Can you believe they hooked up again after the tell all?"

A blink. "Seriously?"

"Oh, yee of little Reddit time." She pats my hand. "I have *all* the dirt." A beat. "Please tell me this means that we're starting a regular trash TV watch party so I can share my knowledge."

"As long as you promise to teach me to crochet."

Those brows shoot up. "*You* want to learn to crochet?"

"I keep seeing those adorable kits on social media, but have never had an excuse to buy one." I shrug. "You'll give me that excuse."

"Oh," she says, rubbing her hands together. "This is good. Very good."

"Is that a yes?"

She lifts her palm for me to smack. "It's a hell yes!"

We high-five, but our celebration is cut short when a puck

ricochets off the glass. Jumping, I glare at Damon through the plexiglass.

He's smirking, clearly proud of startling us both.

"We're plotting!" Kylie yells. "So you'd better be careful."

That doesn't make his smirk fade. In fact, it only grows as he turns his back on us and goes back to stick-handling.

"Maybe we'll put aside crochet and pick up home decorating," she mutters. "I'm sure we can find some truly reprehensible wallpaper to slap up in his bedroom."

I laugh. "Or maybe we can stick to crocheting and trash TV and"—I raise my voice so I know he can hear it—"*not* sharing our sundaes!"

His head whips around, hot blue eyes connecting with mine.

"Oh," Kylie whispers. "I need to know what that's about."

Turning, I wink at her. "Not without copious amounts of wine."

"I'll take that bet." She laughs.

Then, unable to resist, I blow a kiss at Damon, but as I do it, I notice that Colt is watching us.

No.

He's watching *Kylie* laugh.

And his face...

Right.

Well, that might be a problem.

It's a problem for another day, though, I think as I loop my arm through Kylie's and direct us back down the hall. "Let me grab my phone so we can find a day that works for our schedules."

Thankfully, that process doesn't take long, and before I know it, my first Girls' Night in ages is on the books and I'm walking Kylie to her car.

"Damon and I were going to grab dinner tonight," she says.

"Oh, shoot." I hitch my thumb over my shoulder. "Do you want me to grab him?"

"No." She gives me a quick hug, unlocks her car. "Let him have his fun. Plus"—she smiles at me as she tugs open the driver's side door—"I have it on good authority that Damon's not going to be coming home tonight."

Then, with a wink, she's in her car.

And driving away.

THIRTY-TWO

Damon

THE TEAM IS IN SEATTLE, but I'm not with them.

I flew ahead to Vancouver, meeting with another agent—though, thankfully, in person this time instead of on the fucking phone—and then watching some scores come in.

It was one of those weird days where I had both a lot of shit to do and yet a lot of downtime.

The meeting was short.

The scores rolled in without compunction.

The emails and questions I needed to answer were easy to handle.

But as the downtime grew, so did my edginess.

I hate days like this. The moment I let my guard down, shit will hit the fan and then I'll be spending hours putting out fires...all while talking on the fucking phone.

Now, though, I'm chilling in my hotel room, wishing that I wasn't here, but in Seattle, invading Joey's.

Of course, she wouldn't actually be there.

Puck drop is in less than an hour, but instead of watching the game from a box, I'll be well...watching it *on* a box—the flat screen in my room.

"Lame," I mutter, kicking off my shoes and leaning back on the bed.

Which is the exact moment my phone rings.

"Fucking hell." I snag it from the bed, see that it's the legal department calling, and groan.

I don't want to deal with this shit.

And it's definitely going to be shit.

"Dammit." I consider hurling my phone across the room—at least if it's broken I'll get a reprieve from some of the calls—but it's my job, so I resist and begrudgingly swipe my finger across the screen. As it connects, I lift it to my ear and listen for approximately three-point-three seconds before I'm ready to chuck it right out the fucking window, permanently sealed for safety or not.

"Damon, it's Tera."

My newly appointed head of legal sounds like she's about to ask me for a favor I know I'm not going to like.

God dammit.

"Yeah," I mutter. "I know. What do you need?"

She sighs—and yup, this is going to be bad.

"What?" I press.

"Hiller."

A bucket of cold water washes over me. "What the fuck about that fucking asshole?"

"The prosecution wants to drop the case."

That bucket of water turns into a goddamned waterfall. "What the fuck?" I snap. "We have sworn affidavits from a half-dozen guys, along with Ivy, Claire, and Ava. And me. Plus, I sat down and filmed a fucking deposition detailing exactly what I saw, and you're telling me that's not enough?"

"I'm telling you that the prosecution wants to drop the case."

I grind my teeth together, the nightmare days of what happened to Kylie, the guy getting off, all that happened afterward welling up and choking me.

"We have all of that," I manage to grit out. "And it's not fucking enough?"

Tera sighs. "I've offered all assistance necessary to the prosecutor, interns to research and help with filings, funding, fucking coffee and lunch deliveries, but he's not convinced he can win this. At best, he wants to float a fucking plea bargain with no teeth. At worst…"

"He wants to let it all go," I supply.

"Yeah."

"Fuck," I mutter. God, this is exactly the same shit that happened to Kylie.

"I know."

"So what's our next move?"

She sighs. "I'll keep pushing the prosecutor, but we need something else, Damon."

My stomach starts churning.

Because I know something else that would help—

And I will never—fucking *never*—offer it up.

"What kind of something else?" I rasp.

"More people who can come forward with evidence of misconduct—sexual or otherwise. They can be anonymous reports or something that's workplace related. How was he with the coaching staff that remained? Have Joey or Tommy or Dave reported anything?"

Yes.

But fucking *no*.

"Damon?"

I blink, realize I didn't reply and manage to grit out, "No." A silent breath as my mind spins, remembering the hell that Kylie went through, a hell that was completely for naught. "No," I repeat. "I haven't heard anything from them, but I'll check in." Another breath, one that helps me begin thinking clearly. "Let's also go back through his employment record. If he did this with the Sierra, then there are likely victims from his other teams before who can add to the prosecutor's case."

"Likely the statute of limitations has passed on most of those," Tera says.

"It's ten years in California." I clench the phone hard enough for it to creak in protest. "He was only with the Sierra for five. That still leaves time for us to find something."

"That's a good idea," Tera murmurs. "I'll get the team on it."

"I'll let you know if I hear anything from the coaching staff."

Anything except for—

I slam the door shut in my mind, say goodbye, and we hang up.

I sit in silence for a long time, trying to breathe, to calm, to bury that anger inside me again.

It doesn't work.

Eventually, though, I manage to calmly set my phone aside and grab the remote.

Then I turn on the TV and I watch as Joey and the rest of the Sierra win the game.

"Perfect," I mutter. "Fucking perfect."

THE BED BOUNCES SLIGHTLY and I open my eyes.

"Hey, sweetheart," Joey murmurs, pulling the covers back.

God, she's beautiful, and dressed in nothing but one of my tees.

It must be late—really late—considering she and the team had to fly up to Vancouver after their game.

"Hey, Red." I lift a hand, wrap my fingers around her wrist. "Come here."

She comes, crawling into bed next to me, curling up against my side. Sighing, I nuzzle at her hair, loving the scent of her, the feel of her in my arms. "How'd you get in, baby?"

"Shh," she says. "It's the middle of the night. We can talk about my breaking and entering skills later."

My lips curve, but then they flatten out again.

Because I remember that fucking phone call.

Remember that the case against Hiller is fucked and that she might have to deal with the bastard going free—

"Damon?" She rolls over, hand settling on my chest. "What's wrong?"

I realize I've gone stiff.

It takes nearly everything in me to relax my body. I smooth back her hair, press a kiss to her forehead. "Nothing, baby."

"Sweetheart—"

A pulse through my middle, worry gnawing at my bones.

"It's nothing," I lie. "I just remembered the meetings I have tomorrow."

She's still for a long moment, as though gauging that answer for truth.

I brace.

Because it's a fucking lie.

But she doesn't call me on it.

Just presses her lips to my throat and murmurs, "Okay, honey. Then let's get you some rest so you can make it through those meanings."

"Thanks, Red."

She smiles, lips hitting mine for a brief, sweet kiss.

Then I tuck the blankets around us, draw her closer, and settle in to go to sleep.

She's out in minutes.

But it takes me much, much longer.

THIRTY-THREE

Joey

I'M FROWNING as Damon excuses himself from the table, lifting his phone to his ear, trademark scowl in place.

"He's off," Kylie says and I glance over at her, see that her eyebrows are drawn together, worry written into the lines of her face.

"Yes," I agree. "Something's off." I wrinkle my nose. "But he's not talking to me about it."

It's been a week since I first crawled into bed with him in Vancouver, a week since I sensed that tension in him.

A week during which I've asked him multiple times if he's okay, asked him multiple times to talk to me about whatever it is that's clearly bothering him—and all of those asks have gone unanswered.

Or well, the only answer I've been getting is that he's busy but otherwise fine.

But sometimes I catch him looking at me like...

Like he's living a nightmare.

While I'm living a fantasy.

I rub my hand over my chest, trying to soothe the ache there.

But it doesn't help.

Kylie sighs, putting down her fork and reaching across the table to squeeze my arm. "He can be stubborn like that."

"As his sister, do you have any insights about how to break through all of that stubborn?"

She chuckles. "Don't I wish." She squeezes my arm one more time then draws back and returns to her pancakes. "If it's any consolation, these moods of his don't last very long. He'll shake it off and be the Damon of old in no time."

I look out the window, watch as he paces, his phone pressed to his ear.

And I can't beat back the feeling that for all that's good between us, all that feels like everything—and more—I've ever dreamed of, I'm still waiting for it to all go bad, for the other shoe to drop, for...

"Damon mentioned that you had a meeting with Cal."

I jerk, gaze swiveling from the man who practically owns my heart to his sister, who's quickly making her own place in it. "Yeah, I did." Cal's the team's owner and I met with him a couple of days ago to disclose that Damon and I are dating.

"How'd it go?"

My response...is a sigh.

She winces. "That good, huh?"

"Well, I still have a job," I hedge. "And HR did their thing, so we're covered."

"Eh." She waves a hand. "With your record and the health of the team, did you expect anything different?"

"Considering that Hiller was fired for inappropriate conduct and I'm banging the GM...I thought it was a possibility." But I hold myself to a high standard and Damon and I are...well, I hope that we're something that's going to be around for a good long while—despite his moodiness of late—so I knew I needed to have that awkward conversation with Cal.

The press hasn't picked up on our relationship yet.

But Colt has, and obviously so has Storm, and I know the rest of the guys haven't missed it either.

The only reason I'm not getting shit is because I can bench them.

Sooner or later, though, I know the teasing will be coming my way.

It's the way of the hockey world.

"Okay, for one"—she shovels a bite of pancake into her mouth, her next words slightly garbled—"please don't discuss banging and my brother. For another, nothing about you and Damon can compare to the awful shit that Hiller did."

My teeth clamp together, and she curses softly.

"Damn," she says again. "I'm sorry."

"It's—" I shake my head. "I'm fine. It's in the past—" But even as I want to push out the rest of the half-truth, the words stopper up in my throat.

"Yeah." She sighs. "That doesn't work all that well for me either."

I hate that she knows that.

Almost as much as I hate the fact that she can see right through me.

"What does?" I ask.

"What?"

"What works for you?" I ask. "I did the therapy thing. I've put in the work, and sometimes..." I sigh and shrug helplessly.

"Sometimes it's there anyway," she murmurs, sitting back in her chair, pushing her pancakes away. "Truthfully?"

I nod.

"For a long time, nothing helped. Especially when Damon was serving time for me."

Damn. "Shit, Kylie," I whisper. "I shouldn't have brought this up—"

"No." Her eyes are damp and she shakes her head, her hand finding mine. "This is good. I hate pretending everything is perfect all the time." A long, shaky breath. "Because, truthfully, even after Damon's sentence was up and he was going back to living his life, I still wasn't ready to get out there."

"I'm sorry."

"Don't be." She exhales, sits back. "Because even though it took time, even though it took a *long* time, I can tell you that it eventually changes, that life gets better, becomes normal again. Yes, there are blips were the memories pop up, the grief takes over, but they...fade, I guess. Or maybe it's that I've become stronger, so they're easier to deal with."

My lungs spasm. My eyes burn.

But I think about my childhood.

I think about Beth and John and the years after.

I think about sharp pain growing dull and achy, slowly, incrementally, day by day by *day*.

I nod. "You're right," I whisper.

Her smile is sad, but her eyes tell me enough.

She knows I'm telling the truth when I agree with her.

"But you know what makes everything get better faster?" she asks.

"No." I shake my head. "What makes it better faster?"

She shoves my plate toward me. "Pancakes. But also"—her expression softens—"having someone to talk about it with."

Now I know *she's* telling the truth.

Because the dark secret that had been eating away at me for so long is out in the open—or well, it's not completely hidden any longer. It's not just me sharing with my therapist. Kylie knows and Damon knows, and maybe it wouldn't be the worst if my truth was out there in the world. Maybe people wouldn't look at me like I'm broken.

Because I know that Kylie isn't. She's so damned strong, it fills me with pride.

So...why can't I be that strong too?

The chair next to me slides out with a *screech* and I turn to watch Damon sink down next to me.

"All good?"

He glances as me, mouth turned up into a smile I both love and hate. Because his expression is soft but his eyes are distant. "All good, Red." A beat. "Except for the fucking phone calls."

I bump his shoulder with mine, try to coax a real smile out of him. "Burden of being the big boss?"

"Exactly." He tucks my hair behind my ear, leans in and presses a kiss to the hinge of my jaw. "Eat your food, baby."

I pick up my fork, oblige the soft order, but as the meal goes on, I don't miss that he doesn't touch his plate of French toast, barely sips at his mug of hot coffee.

Mostly, he broods.

And even though I give him the sass he loves and Kylie chatters away, her cheery brightness seemingly impossible to dim—even in the face of all her brother's brooding—nothing breaks through.

Something I know she doesn't miss it because her eyes keep coming to mine then sliding to her brother.

Who replies at all the right times.

But isn't engaged in this conversation at all.

Something is definitely up.

And I need to figure out exactly what the hell it is.

Kylie lifts her brows and I shrug slightly. I have no clue how to fix this. I've barely begun to fix myself.

Her blue eyes, so much like Damon's, turn shrewd.

Even before the words come out of her mouth, I know her brother isn't going to like them.

I also know she isn't going to hold them back on his account.

Because she announces, "...and that's not even the best news because guess what?"

I brace, hold myself perfectly still.

Damon sets his coffee down, seems to do the same exact thing I'm doing.

Kylie, meanwhile, just smiles wide, beams of sunshine practically filling up the breakfast restaurant, and blithely continues on,

"I'm moving out!"

My mouth drops open.

And I watch Damon's already dark expression grow even darker.

THIRTY-FOUR

Damon

"I TOLD YOU," I snap. "There's nothing there."

Tera sighs and shoves a hand through her ponytail. "Damn." She allows her arm to drop to the side and shakes her head. "I think that's it then. The asshole is going to get off."

I curse. "The plea deal?"

"Misdemeanors in exchange for time served."

I curse again, barely resisting the urge to pound my fist against the wall. No, to punch it *through* the wall. But I manage to do some box breathing, some visualization—mostly of me turning Hiller into a bloody pulp, and in doing so, I contain my anger. "Any word from the other teams?" I grind out.

She shakes her head again.

My anger banks further, and I focus back on trying to fix this fucked-up mess. "Okay," I say on a staccato breath. "You think you can buy us some time with the district attorney while we keep working on those other teams?"

A wince. "Not much time, but I think I can get a little."

"Good." I shove my hands into my pockets. "Run with that. I'll press the other teams."

She nods and leaves, and I'm alone in my office with thoughts I don't want to have. If Joey just—

No.

This time I lose hold on my temper and my fist collides with the wall with a crash.

Fucking *no.*

Joey doesn't want to do it, so she's not going to fucking do it. Not today. Not fucking ever.

And I'm not going to ask her, going to make her.

She's been through enough.

Because I know if she hears that the case is going to shit, she'll step up, will sacrifice herself without a second thought.

I can't let that happen. I *won't.*

I didn't protect Kylie, didn't protect Joey from what happened, but I can damned well protect her now.

I *have* to.

There's a knock at the door, and I shake my hand out, brush away the Sheetrock dust. Then I shift the file cabinet slightly to hide the new goddamned hole in my wall.

Knock. Knock. Knock.

"Dammit," I mutter, closing my eyes for a heartbeat. Then I take another breath. Calm. Steady.

Then I move to the door and pull it open.

Kylie's standing on the other side with Joey behind her, who's wearing an expression I've seen too many times over the last couple of weeks.

Worry.

No matter how hard I try to hide it, she's still picking up on my tension.

I need to talk to her, put her at ease.

I just...need a solution for this fucked-up mess first.

"What's up?" I ask, surveying the twosome who have gotten close.

Close enough to have a couple of Girls' Nights that saw me kicked out of my house for the evening. Close enough that they gang up on me.

"Joey has practice," Kylie says as she and Joey step into my office and shut the door. "But we went shopping this morning—"

See?

A terrible twosome who drink wine, crochet terribly, watch inane TV shows, and apparently, go shopping.

"What for?" I ask.

My sister claps her hands together. "I have a new apartment to decorate!"

I scowl.

Which, because my sister lives to torment me, makes her smile. She pats my chest. "It was only a matter of time, honey."

My scowl deepens. "I have plenty of space. There's no need for you to move out."

"Regardless," she says. "I am."

"Kylie—"

"Well," Joey interjects. "On the note of that now painfully familiar argument, I'll leave you to your torture." Her fingers find mine, wrap tight, holding me in place as her eyes search my face for several moments. Then she shakes her head slightly, lips curving up into a sad smile. "So I can get on with enacting my own."

"Get it, girl," Kylie says.

Smile turning warm, Joey lifts up on tiptoe and presses her lips to my jaw.

I feel that deep, soothing the rough edges inside me.

She's been careful about the PDA here at the rink—not because the guys haven't picked up on the change in our relationship. They have—of course they have. They're smart and gossip spreads through the organization like pollen on a windy, spring day, especially after she met with Cal...and then Cal met with me, giving us the...

Well, not really the *okay* so much as the not going to shitcan us for doing something that's frowned upon.

Luckily, consent is a thing.

Along with a winning record and playoff experience.

Still, we're not exactly throwing it in anyone's face.

But we're not exactly hiding it either.

"Have fun, Red," I tell her.

Another long, searching gaze.

Then she squeezes Kylie's arm and slips from the room.

When the door closes with a soft click, my sister turns back to me, accusation in her blue eyes. "You promised me you'd make it better. Not worse."

I still, those words slicing through me like a sharp blade. "Kylie," I rasp.

"What are you hiding?"

I sigh. "Nothing."

"Liar." She shoves lightly at my chest. "I can deal with you hiding stuff from me—I get it. You're the overprotective older brother, but that doesn't work in a relationship, Damon. It just *doesn't.*"

"And what would *you* know about a relationship?" I snap.

Her inhalation is sharp, but not as sharp as the pain in her eyes.

"Shit, Kylie," I say quickly. "I didn't mean that. I'm an asshole. I-I—"

Fuck.

I'm fucking this up.

It's just...it's this goddamned secret and my fucking temper and—

"I'm sorry," I tell her. "I shouldn't have said that."

"No, you shouldn't have." She sighs and it's heavy. "If I didn't already know that something is seriously wrong then that right there would have told me." She touches my chest. "What's going on? I haven't seen you like this since—" Her throat works. "Since I was hurt."

"Kylie, I—"

"Tell me."

"There's nothing to—"

"*Tell* me."

"I—"

"Damon. *Just* tell me."

"Don't we have curtains or some shit to install at your new place? Throw pillows to fluff? A bed frame to put together—"

"Tell me."

"The back of the trunk is probably full of shit I need to schlep up to your place. We should go and get that done. I fly out tomorrow for that scouting trip, so if we don't do it today then it'll have to wait until the end of the week—"

"*Tell me.*"

Fuck. *Fuck.*

"And then you'll be doing all that heavy lifting yourself—"

"Damon," she says quietly. "You need to cut this out. Just...stop trying to bury this shit and *tell* me the freaking truth."

I can't.

I *can't.*

I've failed in so many ways.

I can't fail in this too.

"For me," she whispers, her eyes filling with tears. "Stop

trying to protect me from whatever this is and please just trust me to be able to help you handle it."

"I can't—"

Her face falls.

And I can't stand it, can't stand her thinking that I don't trust her.

"Hiller's going to get off."

THIRTY-FIVE

Joey

"OH, MY GOD!" Kylie says, later that night. "She did *not* just throw her shoe at him."

My eyes are wide, but I'm glued to the TV screen as another sparkly pump goes flying. "I thought they get in trouble if they're violent."

"I mean, Reddit says that's in their contract, but I think they care more about good TV than anything else so…"

"And now I feel icky." I wrinkle my nose and grab a handful of popcorn, shove it in my mouth to cure the guilt I'm curating for watching shows that likely take advantage of their cast members.

"In fairness to that moral code of yours I see has been piqued," Kylie murmurs. "I think the people on this particular show also care about good TV more than anything else—well, that and getting peeps over to their OnlyFans."

My brows flick up. "That's an awfully cynical take."

She sighs, shrugs. "Well, I find that I'm feeling more than a little cynical tonight."

I snag the remote, hit pause. "Spill."

"Ignore me," she says. "I'm tired from moving all day—"

"And shopping," I add, trying to get her to smile.

It works, but it's not a real smile.

Damn.

"And shopping," she murmurs. Her gaze is on her glass, and I watch the liquid slosh slightly as she slowly spins the stem between thumb and forefinger. "Anyway, this is supposed to be a celebration. You and the team are leaving in a couple of days, Damon's doing the same tomorrow, zipping around the country, doing GM things before catching up with you, and I'm"— she lifts the back of her hand to her forehead—"the poor soul who's going to be left all alone."

I nudge her knee with mine. "Nice try. Your social calendar is busier than my work one."

"Nah, that's just because you're an introvert who likes to spend an inordinate amount of time in your bathtub—"

I don't mention that her brother is responsible for my growing love for bathtubs, nor the talents he displays for drawing out my pleasure while I'm soaking in them.

No need to scar her.

"—I'm going to be all alone." A beleaguered sigh. "So very alone."

"Is this you trying to get an invitation to our trip to New York?"

She waggles her brows. "Is there shopping in New York?"

I steal her wine glass, down the last inch of chardonnay (we've gone through our stock for this evening).

"Hey!"

I set it on the table then turn to face her, fixing her in place with my most intense Coach Stare—the one that never fails to get my players to spill their guts. "Tell me," I order quietly.

"That you can have my wine?" A scowl. "Fine. You can have my wine." A beat. "Even though it's already in your stomach."

"Kylie, honey, please just talk to me."

Her eyes cut to the side, avoiding mine for a long moment.

Then she sighs and looks back at me, her blue eyes piercing into mine. "If I promise to tell you, I need you to promise me something in return."

Heart skipping a beat, I take her hand. "I promise."

She sighs, eyes drifting away and back again. Then she says something that has the bottom dropping out of my world.

"Hiller's going to get away with it."

"Please don't leave," Kylie says as she follows me out to the parking lot of the apartment complex.

My head is spinning.

And it's spinning not because Hiller might get away with it, not because that's a reality that happens far too often, and not even because the shadows of that night haven't completely left my life.

It's spinning because of Damon.

Because he's known.

And he didn't fucking *tell* me.

I don't know what to do with that information.

I don't know how to *recover* from the blow of it.

I can handle him being protective of me, I can even handle that straying into *over*protective. But hiding the truth from me, waiting until there might not be anything for me to do to stop this shit from happening, putting me off time and again when I've asked him what's wrong...

God, he knows I don't trust easily.

He knows *everything* about my past.

And he's lying to me.

Gaslighting me.

What the *actual* fuck?

"Joey—"

I turn back to Kylie and pull her into a tight hug. I hate that she's trembling, that she's clearly worried she's messed up in telling me. "It's going to be okay," I promise her, grasping on to my calm by the very edges of my fingertips, barely able to keep my voice steady. "I just need a little time to think about what I want to do—"

Those eyes flare with worry. "About Damon? He didn't mean—"

I touch her cheek, swiping away a tear that's slid down her face. "About Hiller, honey."

More tears escape. "I don't want you to have to—"

I pull her close again. "I know. It's a shit thing. We both know it. We've both lived it. But..." The truth settles deep inside me. "This isn't just about me or you. This is about all of us. So as painful as it is for me to think of it, to talk about it, to move on from it"—I pull back, holding her by the tops of her shoulders—"we're not in the shadows anymore. They don't have power over us any longer. *You* helped me find that, remember? So don't go and forget it now."

Her lungs hitch. "Damon's trying to protect you."

My eyes close and I focus on breathing steady, on thinking beyond my frustration and hurt. Then I peel back my lids and hold her stare. "I know," I tell her. "Please don't worry. I understand that."

Does it change anything? Does that make it better?

I'm not sure in this moment.

But I don't tell Kylie that, don't give her something else to worry about.

I just wipe her tears from her cheeks and hug her again.

Then I get in my car and drive to my office at the rink.

On the way, I call Tera—the head of legal who took over after everything went down with Hiller—at home.

It's far too late for a pleasant chat, something I know that *she* knows immediately because her tone is all business when she asks, "What's wrong?"

"Hiller's going to get off?" I ask quietly.

There's a long blip of quiet.

Then, "Damon didn't talk to you?"

No. Because he remembered what I said, knew I didn't want my legacy to be that of a victim, thought he was shielding me from—

I exhale sharply then focus. "Please just explain."

She does—about the district attorney thinking the case won't look good at trial, that a jury will be unlikely to issue a conviction. "He wants to offer a plea deal that means he'll skate with just time served."

Meaning the couple of days he spent in jail before bail was made.

My temple throbs as I absorb that blow.

Then I sigh and know I have to make a decision.

Or maybe...I made the decision the moment my car pointed me in the direction of the rink instead of home.

"It's bullshit," Tera says. "The same sort of misogyny that has made it so men don't face consequences for their actions time and again." She sighs. "And there's nothing we can do about it—I've contacted past employers, pressed the D.A., hired private investigators, talked to all of our staff again—"

"Except me."

There's a long blip of quiet.

"Joey?"

"You've talked to all of the staff except for *me*."

More silence. Then, "Damon told me he spoke to all of the coaches."

"He might have spoken to the rest of the coaching staff," I say quietly. "But he didn't speak to me."

Her inhalation rattles through the speaker, and it takes everything in me to press on.

But I do.

"Because he already knew that Hiller raped me."

THIRTY-SIX

Damon

I FROWN as I walk to my car, not quite comprehending what I'm seeing.

Joey's car in the lot.

She's supposed to be with Kylie, drinking wine, watching crap TV, and then calling me so I can pick her up and we can try out drunk sex.

Instead...

I stride over to the spot, peer in through the window and see the picture one of her young fans drew for her tucked behind the gearshift, and know it's her car.

"What the hell?" I mutter.

I pull out my phone, see that Kylie's called and left me a message, but just pocket it again and head for the rink.

Maybe Joey got caught up with something and lost track of time.

I'll pop in and make sure that she's all good, drive her over to Kylie's if they still want to meet up.

Then we don't have to worry about leaving her car at the apartment complex.

Grinning, I grab my badge, scan into the building, and make my way through the corridors until I get to Joey's office. The light is on, but it's empty, her purse on the desk, her laptop bag beside it.

"Hmm," I mutter turning for the kitchen.

Maybe she went to grab something to eat.

But the kitchen proves to be empty as well.

And the locker room, the conference rooms, the training suite and cool and hot plunge rooms. No one is here except for housekeeping and maintenance staff.

Then I hear a noise.

It's familiar and not and it drives me out through the doors that lead to the rink.

I inhale sharply when I see her, skates on, stick in hand.

I climb up to the bench, lean against the boards, and watch her. She doesn't have full mobility in the knee that ended her college career, but she's graceful and powerful, using compact strides and stick-handling that isn't showy. Still, it's effective as she skates through the neutral zone, dances along the blue line then streaks in, fires a shot on goal.

It hits the top corner and then she moves in and swoops up the rebound.

But she's doing it without really thinking, her movements automatic, almost robotic.

Another carry of the puck, another shot, this one misses wide and she scoops it up again, carries it to the face-off dot, weaving in and out, back and forth.

This time she hits that corner again, but she does it with a wince, limping slightly as she retrieves the puck then starts up again.

But this time, she stops, her gaze coming up, arrowing toward...

Me.

Her expression is unreadable for a long moment and I'm about to call out, to apologize for startling her, but then she smiles and skates my way.

"Knee bothering you?" I ask as she comes close.

One slender shoulder lifts and drops. "No more than normal."

"You forget about Kylie?"

"No," she says. "We hung out for a bit, but I remembered I left my computer, so I popped over to get it after the first episode." She shrugs again, mouth curving. "Then I guess...I just had the itch to get out here and mess around."

"Well, for all your messing around, that shot of yours looks pretty damned good, Red."

She grins. "The knee holds up for that one." She winces. "Though not for much longer." A jerk of her chin. "I should get these skates off."

"You want a ride back to Kylie's?" I offer. "I can pick you up when you're done."

"We're done for the night." She climbs over the boards, starts for the hall and I follow her. "I'm probably just going to go home."

My brows drag together. "You're going to go home? What happened to coming to my place?"

She stills. "Oh, I just thought since you were flying out tomorrow and it's late—"

"I want you there." A beat. "With me. For however long I can have you."

Her eyes search mine for long enough that my nape begins to prickle, but then she smiles. "Even if it means missing sleep?"

"Oh"—I slip an arm around her middle—"it will *definitely* mean missing sleep." I press my lips to her temple. "But it will also definitely be worth it."

She chuckles. "Can't say you're wrong." Then she's shifting out of my hold, striding to her office. It only takes a couple of minutes to get her skates off, but she's quiet during that time.

"You okay, Red?" I ask as she puts the guards on.

"Hmm?" she asks, shoving the skates into a duffle bag and setting it on the edge of her desk.

"Baby"—I catch her hand—"are you okay?"

"What?" She shakes herself. "I'm fine."

"You're a million miles away." I tuck her hair behind her ear. "You've barely looked at me since you came off the ice."

"I'm sorry." She touches my jaw, eyes filled with that apology before she grimaces. "I'm distracted. My mind is going a hundred miles an hour getting ready for the road trip." A sigh. "Especially with Knox's ankle bothering him." Her fingers wrap around mine before she smiles. "But I'm glad you're here so I can stop going around and around about it."

"Do you want to talk about lines for tomorrow?"

"No." She says it a little too quickly, but before I can call her on it, she snags her bag and comes close again. "I'd rather just go home and have you distract me." Her mouth curves. "Think you can handle that, hot shot?"

My dick twitches. "I think I can be *convinced* to handle it."

"Good," she whispers.

I snag her bag. "Need anything else?"

"No."

I jerk my chin to the hall. "Then let's get on with the distracting."

We make our way through the corridor then out into the night air, but as we move to my car, she peels off to hers. "I'll meet you at your place?"

"Do you want me to drive—?" My phone buzzes, cutting me off.

"I'll follow you over." She presses her lips to mine. "Answer your phone." Her mouth quirks. "Because I know that's your favorite thing."

"Baby—"

"Go on." She drops back to her heels, moves to her car and I hear the locks disengage.

I pull my phone out, see that Kylie has texted.

> KYLIE: Are you and Joey okay?

> DAMON: We're fine. We met up at the rink. Why?

I see the "..." appear and then disappear a few times and my stomach sinks.

"All good?" Joey asks, poised in her open driver's side door.

My phone buzzes again, but I ignore it for a moment. "All good."

She grins. "Good."

I look down at my phone screen again.

> KYLIE: Good. I wanted to make sure you two connected.

> DAMON: We did and now we're heading back to the house. Need anything?

> KYLIE: I'm all set.

"Am I racing you to your place?" Joey calls.

I glance up to see her smiling, but I'm distracted from the fact that it's not completely normal when my cell vibrates again.

> KYLIE: I love you, big bro. Don't ever forget that.

My eyes narrow and I start to type out a reply.

But then I hear Joey's car door slam, her engine start up, and I pocket my phone.

I'll text my sister back later.

For now, I have a race to win.

"Oʜ, Goᴅ!" she moans, head dropping back, water splashing over the edges of the tub.

That'll be a fucking mess to clean up later, but I don't give a damn.

Not with that gorgeous cunt of hers squeezing me tight, not with her grinding against me, hard and fast and driving me up to the edge—

Then over.

I grunt, fingers tightening on her hips, keeping her moving on my dick as she begins to slow, her orgasm leaving her limp as mine crests.

Fucking perfect.

Fucking best ever.

"*Fuck*," I groan, head falling back against the tile.

She collapses against my chest, breathing heavy, arms wrapped around me.

We lay there for long enough that I realize the water's getting cold. I hit the lever with my foot, start draining the tub.

"Bedtime, Red."

Her breathing stays even and she doesn't move.

I gently brush back her hair. "Time to get out, baby."

She moans softly and I grin, lifting her and carefully stepping out of the tub. She's practically limp as I towel her off, eyes closed, her replies mumbled and sleepy.

I tug a tee over her head then tuck her under the covers. "Sleep now, baby."

"Thanks, sweetheart," she slurs.

I go and take care of the water that sloshed on the tile, dump the dirty towels into the hamper then crawl into bed next to her and let sleep take me under.

It's not until later that I realize her *sweetheart* sounded off.

Sounded *wrong*.

Just like her smile at the rink.

And not because she was tired.

But because something *was* wrong.

Seriously fucking *wrong*.

THIRTY-SEVEN

Joey

I SLIP out of the house, exhausted from not having slept, but also not having trusted myself to wake up in time.

To wake up before him.

I need to get the hell out of here.

Now.

I close the front door softly behind me, hit the button on the keypad to engage the lock then slip out to my car, tense until I'm out of the driveway and down the street.

No morning skate today, and I take full advantage of that. Instead of heading to the rink, I make a pitstop by my house to get my things for tonight then drive up through the winding roads, getting lost in the trees, in the morning sunshine.

I don't stop.

Not when my phone rings.

Not as the road gets narrower.

Not until I'm at the top of the mountain.

Only then do I pull to a stop, slotting my car into an opening on the side of the road.

For a long time, I stare out at the vista in front of me—acres and acres of pine trees, the gorgeous blue lake in the distance.

And I prepare myself.

For what I'm going to do.

For what I *have* to do.

Can I?

Do I have a choice?

I do...but I don't.

Because it's not just about me. It's about everyone before and everyone after and—

Yeah, it's also about me.

I exhale as I stare out at the grand expanse of mountains, the evidence of the beauty of nature and the truth that I'm only a very tiny piece in all the vastness of the universe...and I make a decision.

No.

I accept the decision I've already made.

My phone buzzes for the umpteenth time—apparently at this elevation, cell service has a clear shot to torment me. I glance down and read another text from Damon, see that the chain of messages are growing ever more concerned.

Guilt ripples through me, but although I spent the last eighteen hours thinking, wondering, worrying, I still haven't figured that part out, haven't figured out what I'm going to do about Damon.

I love him.

I have for a while.

But can I be in a relationship with someone who kept something like this from me?

Even as that question buzzes along my mind, I can't keep

out the ironic realization that I'm doing the same exact thing as he did right now.

Keeping something from Damon to protect *him*.

My head pulses with pain, with the dissonance, with the hurt.

Then I tuck it all away.

Because I can't deal with that right now.

I need to confront what happened with Hiller, my failures afterward, my guilt from not speaking up...

And that's more than my fair share already.

In fact, it feels like so much of a fucking share that my lungs are tight, my thoughts spin with all the speed of a hurricane, and my heart feels shredded.

But I can handle this.

God knows, I've handled so much more.

So I stand there, focusing on my breath, on the untouched nature in front of me.

Green pines. Granite mountains. A blue, blue lake.

Slow and steady breaths. A cool breeze on my sweat-coated skin.

And eventually, I'm able to come out of that whirlwind, to be at peace with my decision, and then, long minutes later, to type out a reply to Damon.

> JOEY: I'm fine. I'll explain later tonight. Call me after you land.

It's mere seconds later when my cell buzzes with a reply.

> DAMON: I rescheduled my flight. Where are you? Let's talk now.

> JOEY: I'll call you later.

He replies again, but I don't read it, certainly don't answer it.

I just let that boundary stand...because I can't right now.

Instead, I pull up Tera's contact information and hit the button to call her.

"You ready?" she asks after we exchange greetings.

My blood is freezing in my veins, my spine has gone stiff, and my head is threatening to spin out again, but sure, I'm fine.

Fine. Fine. Everything is *fine.*

Channeling that meme, I exhale one more time, nod even though she can't see me, and say, "I'm ready."

"Okay," she says gently. "Know I'll be with you every step of the way."

"I know."

"Good," she murmurs. "So you'll meet me..." She gives me the address, and I nod again, still knowing she can't see me, but I can't stop myself.

"I'll be there," I whisper.

"Joey?"

"Yeah?"

"You don't have to do this."

My lungs inflate in a rush, bringing oxygen so quickly to my brain that my vision goes hazy for a few seconds. I let a breath out. Take another back in.

Then I say, "I know. But I'm doing it anyway."

I tell her goodbye then hang up.

A moment later, I'm making my way back to my car and heading down the mountain.

I meet up with Tera, with the district attorney and the detective handling Hiller's case...and I keep my promise.

To the other women.

And to myself.

THIRTY-EIGHT

Damon

"I THOUGHT you were flying out this morning."

I turn, tear my gaze away from the guys warming up below, and see Kylie hovering in the doorway of the owner's box.

"I changed my flight."

She nibbles at her bottom lip. "Because of what happened with Joey?"

My head jerks and I set my tablet aside. "What happened with Joey?"

"What do you mean?" She frowns. "You said you talked to her last night and everything was fine."

I push out of my chair, move to the back of the suite, tugging her fully inside and out of view of any errant cameras, then close the door behind her.

"Ky," I say, the edges of my temper fraying. "I need you to spell it out for me, babe."

"I..." Worry skitters across my sister's face.

"Tell me," I order quietly.

Carefully.

Catching those frayed edges, clinging to them desperately to keep them contained.

"She knows about Hiller's case going bad."

My heart spasms, my hold on those strands slipping. "What?" I rasp.

Kylie reaches for me, but I step back. "Damon," she whispers.

I think about Joey on the ice last night, think about that sad, tortured smile in the parking lot. I think about the bath, the weird *sweetheart* that sounded like a goodbye, think about going to sleep with her in my arms...

And then I think about waking up alone in my empty bed.

"Fuck!"

"I didn't mean to tell her," she says in a rush. "I know you were trying to protect her and that eventually you would talk to her, but she saw something was wrong with me and then I couldn't hold it in and—and—" A tear slips down her cheek. "We were talking and it just came out. I think she's okay," she adds in a hurry. "We've been working through our...stuff together and we've been talking and..."

"Kylie."

"It's been good. Helpful for both of us. But I still wanted to check in with you guys, so when you said it was fine..." She lifts a shaky hand to her forehead. "I'm sorry. I never should have—"

"Ky."

"Really," she says. "I'll talk to her, make sure she knows that it's not your fault—"

I close my eyes, exhale, trying to shove down the red haze at the edges of my vision, to keep control of my temper.

Fuck, after all I've done for my sister, she told Joey—

No.

Not after all *I've* done. I didn't almost kill that mother-fucker because of Kylie—or not entirely anyway.

It was me, my anger, my inability to protect her from what was done to her.

"Don't worry," she says, dropping her hand to her side and coming close, staring at me with earnest blue eyes. "I'll fix this. I promise, I'll fix it."

I open my mouth to tell her that I've got it.

But I don't get the words out.

Because the lights go down and the national anthem plays and then the puck drops.

And she doesn't have time to fix it.

And neither do I.

OVER THE NEXT three hours I manage to convince Kylie that I'm not mad, that I'll handle Joey—with care—and that every-thing is going to be fine.

The Sierra win handily, but between all that convincing and the anger gnawing at my insides (how could she not fucking talk to me, how could she skip out this morning, how could she leave me in the dark?) I'm hardly paying attention to the action on the ice.

I distantly hear the crowd roar for the Sierra's goals, blearily stare at the Jumbotron to track the score, but it's not at the fore-front of my consciousness.

Not at all.

After the game ends and I've walked Ky to her car, she pauses, snags my hand, squeezing it tight. "Are you sure you're—?"

"I'm sure," I say, nudging her toward the open driver's side door. "I'm fine. It'll all be fine."

"But—"

"Ky," I murmur, "I'll just give her time to wrap up her post-game and then we'll talk."

My sister nibbles at the corner of her mouth.

"I promise."

"I love you," she whispers. "And I'm so—"

"Christ, kid," I grumble, but do it gently because she needs it. "Get out of here and let me fix this."

Her eyes hold mine. "Because you can fix anything."

My lungs spasm, worry eating its way through my temper.

I fucking hope she's right.

"Drive carefully," I tell her. "Then text me when you get home."

She nods and climbs into her car before backing out of the spot and heading for the exit.

Afterward, I stare at the door to the arena, trying to figure out the best way to handle this. When the answer doesn't immediately come, I shake my head. Nothing to do except push forward.

I weave my way through the halls and park my ass in Joey's office.

Her purse and computer are here.

She's not leaving without them.

There's a knock, and I look up, see Tera standing in the cracked door. "She okay?"

My brows drag together.

"Joey," she murmurs, gaze sliding around the room before she shifts inside. "I know she just coached a hell of a game, but talking about what happened to her with the D.A. and detective this morning couldn't have been easy."

Alarm bells blare and I'm barely able to hear Tera's next words.

"Deciding to press charges and then going right back to work"—Tera shakes her head—"I'm in awe of her strength."

Joey is pressing charges?

She talked to the fucking detective and district attorney this morning?

Without me at her side, making sure—

"So, anyway," Tera finishes, "I just wanted to make sure she was fine."

Fine.

Fine.

Everyone's checking in to make sure she's fine.

After she blew up her life and put herself back in Hiller's crosshairs.

My anger ramps.

I'm going to fucking throttle her.

What the hell is she thinking?

Still, Tera's waiting for an answer, so I rasp out, "She's fine." And no, the irony of that lie is not lost on me.

Tera's gaze connects with mine. Then she exhales. "But you're not."

I exhale silently, clench my hands into fists. "I'll deal."

She studies me, as though trying to decide if that's truth or fiction, but all she says is, "You'll let me know if that changes?"

I nod tersely.

Then, thank fuck, she leaves.

And I'm left to stew for the next hour before Joey pushes into her office, her lips parting in surprise. "Damon," she whispers, worry gathering on her face.

I stalk toward her, watching the concern bloom in her eyes. "What the fuck, Red?"

She backs up. "Why are you here?"

"I asked, *what the fuck?*" I growl.

"What the fuck what?" she snaps, chin lifting.

"Hiller." Her green eyes flare. "The district attorney." I bend, my face an inch from hers. "The fucking *detective.*"

She side-steps me, moving to her desk and packing up her things. "Look, I'm not happy that you kept what was happening with the case from me." Her head comes up. "*Really* not happy."

Those threads of my temper, the ones I've been struggling to contain all night...snap.

I stride over to her, but she's still talking.

"But I understand what you've been struggling with, all the feelings this must bring up for you. Do I wish you would have talked to me about it? Yeah, of course I do. Same as I know that I didn't handle my response to finding out what you kept from me well because I did the same thing—I didn't discuss it with you and then I kept what I was going to do in response from you."

"Yeah," I grit out. "You fucking did."

Her expression doesn't waver. "But, the truth is, I needed to do it on my own."

"No, you fucking didn't."

"Damon." She sighs, rubbing a hand over her face. "Look. I get we have a lot to talk about, a lot to work out about how we communicate. But this is an extreme situation and this has been a really long day. A *shit* day. Can we just table this for tonight and talk about everything tomorrow?"

That's reasonable.

Logical.

But the rage I've worked for years to bury, to tame...it's fucking spiraling out of control.

And she's caught in the crossfire.

"No."

She blinks, eyes going wide. "N-no?"

"No. Fucking *no*." I turn away from her, gripping my hair as I try to tamp down my rage.

She talked to—

She *exposed* herself to people who might hurt her, fuck up the career she loves—

No. Hell *fucking* no.

Fury, hot and furious and completely out of control, bursts free.

And then, unbidden of any logic or love, the words just fly out of me, sharp as a knife and just as dangerous. "Christ," I snap, "if this is what it's going to mean to be in a relationship with you, where you don't fucking trust me to protect you, then I don't want it."

There's silence.

Long enough for me to process the idiocy I've just spouted, for my temper to disappear like a puff of smoke.

"Fuck." I spin back to face her. "I didn't—"

But I don't get the chance to let her know *I* know precisely how fucking stupid I am.

Because she says, "You d-don't want it? Don't want *us?*"

"Baby, I—"

My cell rings, and if it was anyone else calling, I would have ignored it.

But it's *Kylie's* ringtone.

And Joey knows it too.

"Pick up your sister's call," she says.

"Red—" I begin.

"Pick up," she orders.

"Red—"

"*Answer it.*"

I take a look at the frozen emerald eyes, the stiffness in her shoulders, the fucking *hurt* in every inch of her body and I know I have to fix this.

I open my mouth—

"Answer. The. *Fucking*. Call. Damon."

Shaking myself, I swipe across the screen, lift the phone to my ear.

And standing there, listening to the sound of my sister's voice, I watch as Joey grabs her bag, her phone, her keys...

And then I watch as she leaves.

THIRTY-NINE

Joey

"MAN," I hear. "Coaching is a tough gig, isn't it?"

I still at the silky voice, the *smug* voice.

I've barely reached the parking lot, my complete focus on just making it to my car when each step feels as though my knees may give way.

Damon said—

Hurt ripples through my abdomen even as I try to slap bandages on the wounds inside me.

Hiding things from me. Not talking to me. Giving me a taste of that trademark temper with words that...

Fucking *hurt.*

So yeah, I haven't exactly been aware of my surroundings.

I don't know if the man—the annoying reporter who's been dogging me for months— followed me or was just waiting in the shadows, preparing to pounce.

All I know is he's here now.

Annoying me.

I exhale, force out my reply through my tight throat. "I'm done with sound bites for the night. Catch me after next game."

"You seem upset."

Clenching my jaw, I don't stop, just keep moving to my car, grabbing the handle on the driver's door. "It's late."

"Is it that?" he drawls. "Or is it that head coaching is really hard on a woman's love life?"

A lance to my heart, stealing all the breath from my lungs.

I release the handle, spin to face the man.

It's not the asshole question. It's not the smugness. It's...the note of something familiar in that condescending tone.

Why do I recognize it?

Why does the young male reporter, his phone in his hand, his—you guessed it—*smug* expression in place, look so fucking familiar?

It's not because I've seen him at press conferences.

It's—

"Hiller," I whisper as horror slides down my spine. I've seen this man before...in a photograph that used to sit on my desk. *Before* it was my desk. When it was Hiller's desk. When I ignored screaming fits and being berated—Hiller's modus operandi for dealing with frustrations.

While trying to do my job. While I sat across from him and tried to pretend the shit that he did to me didn't happen.

While guilt and shame ate at my insides.

The kid's chin comes up and it's then that I fully see his father in the line of his jaw, the hardness in his eyes—like he's a rattlesnake prepared to strike.

He just smiles. "You fuck with my dad, and I fuck with you." He taps on his phone's screen, points it to face me, and...

I watch a shaking video of Damon and me in my office, clearly taken through a sliver of opening, the edge of the door blocking most of the space. But not blocking us. Not blocking

Damon as he paces. Me as my face falls, hurt rippling through my expression—

Fuck, it's worse seeing it like this than experiencing it the first time.

"...if this is what it's going to mean to be in a relationship with you, where you don't fucking trust me to protect you, then I don't want it."

"You d-don't want it? Don't want us?"

"Y-you d-don't w-want i-it?" he sneers. "God how fucking pathetic is it that a sniveling bitch like you is here while my dad got fired? So"—a shrug—"now the world will see exactly who you are." He taps at the screen, shows me what I missed before: that the video of Damon and me is on a popular social media app. "Posted five minutes ago and it already has six thousand views. This shit's going viral, baby." He grins and it's terrible. "This is too fucking perfect. I cannot believe that my dad was fired and you're here *and* you're screwing the GM. That's fucking rich. How many times did you have to blow Damon before you got the job? Ten? Twenty? A hundred?"

I watch this man, this fucking monster in the making and... I'm just done.

He's not, though. "Now that Damon doesn't want you, are you going to ruin his career too?" A smirk. "Or maybe I should have waited to post so I could see what kind of head you would give to get me to delete it."

Something snaps inside me and I decide, *fuck it.*

He shakes his head. "God, all my dad did was—"

"Rape me."

His mouth drops open, his eyes going wide. He's silent for a long moment before he stammers out, "Wh-what did you—?"

I step closer.

Done.

I am so totally fucking done that I react on the fly, pulling out my phone, bringing up the same app he used, and starting a new live video. "A few minutes ago this man"—I turn, getting myself and Hiller's son in the frame as I search my brain for his name—"Zach Hiller," I say as it comes to me, "recorded me without my knowledge during a painful, heartbreaking conversation. Then as I was trying to go home, planning to cry into a glass of wine while I came to terms with the fact that the man I love may not feel the same way, he decided he needed to confront me in the parking lot and rub it in."

I move, cutting him off when he tries to slink away.

"Oh no, Zach," I say, watching as the live count grows. "You wanted to do this, let's do this. You asked how I got the job. You asked if it was because I blew our GM and the man I love, Damon Connors."

"I—"

"You asked if I fucked my way into the position." Yeah, Tera and the legal team are going to kill me, especially when I keep going. But...zero fucks to give right now. "It couldn't be that I'm qualified, right? It couldn't be that I've worked for it. Of course not."

"You—" Rage flashes through his eyes, but I keep going.

"Then you asked why I'm still here when I'm in a relationship with Damon—or *was*, I guess, until tonight," I add flippantly, even though my heart is shredded. "You asked why I'm here, with all that baggage when your dad is gone. And not that I owe you an explanation, but Damon and I are new and—*gasp*—consensual. Plus, Cal, the team's owner for those out there who don't know, and our HR department have both been notified. They weren't thrilled, because of what happened with your dad last season, but the heart wants what the heart wants, right?"

He sniffs.

"And *then* this is where shit gets really real, right? Because you tried to minimize your dad sexually harassing and assaulting multiple women in the organization before he was fired as *all my dad did*—" I shift, point the camera more fully at him. "And do you remember what *I* said?"

He clamps his mouth shut, glances away.

I look to the camera. "I told you that your dad raped me." For a second, I falter. Then I remember Kylie, remember *me*. I can do this. "I don't care if you believe me. I don't care if you think that I had it coming—how dare I be in a male space. I don't even care if it's the only thing you remember about me. Because I endured that, endured your dad's abuse for *years*, and even after he raped me, I hid it. I lived in shame, lived with thinking that maybe I deserved it. So, I let my guilt for not speaking up tear me apart, and I'm done—*done*—with that. Maybe I'll always be that girl hockey coach who was raped, but I know in here"—I drop my free hand to my chest—"that one moment doesn't define me. I'm more than what a man did to me, and if people can't understand that then I just...don't care anymore." I glance over my shoulder at Zach. "Now, kiddo," I say mockingly, "did you have anything *else* to add?"

"Fuck you, bitch," he snaps.

Then he storms off, and I stay live until he gets in his car and screeches out of the lot.

I look back to the camera, stomach churning at the sheer number of people watching—yup, Tera is definitely going to kill me. "I've tried to be perfect," I say quietly to the viewers. "Killed myself to do everything right—and bad things still happened to me. Fault me for falling in love with the wrong person, be pissed because I didn't get us to the Cup last year or messed with your favorite line combination. But please, I'm begging you, know that you're more than what other people try to make you."

I click the button to end the live.

Turn off my phone—this will still be there for me to deal with in the morning.

And then I get in my car and turn on the engine.

I drive carefully—oh so carefully—home, abiding every speed limit, making full and complete stops at every single intersection that requires them, signaling all turns, pulling slowly into my garage.

Holding my breath until the heavy metal door rumbles closed.

Only then do I lose my hold on my tears.

I fumble for the handle, crawl out of my car. I make it to the door to the house, shove it open, whacking my arm on the frame as I stumble through, and...

Only then do I allow my knees to give way.

FORTY

Damon

I PULL up behind Kylie's little SUV, surprised to see another car parked in front of hers.

More surprised to see Colt, suit jacket spread out beneath him as he lies on his back and positions a jack.

Kylie has a flat tire.

In the worst possible place.

It's late. It's dark. The road is narrow.

And she tried to call Triple A but they told her it would be at least an hour before they would make it out to her.

And...

Who the fuck am I kidding?

I used the opportunity to escape the devastation I wrought in Joey. Yeah, she told me to go. But I went because I fucked up royally and I don't know how to fix it, don't know if I *can* fix it.

I'm supposed to protect.

I'm supposed to be better than this—

My car door is tugged open and then my sister is there,

undoing my belt, grabbing my arm and yanking me out of my car. I follow her tugs robotically, distantly take in that Colt is starting in on the lug nuts.

"What happened?" she demands.

I blink, try my best to focus, but my stomach's churning and my head is full of bullshit, and my temper...well, it's so deeply encased in ice that it might be extinguished forever. But even with that small victory, I still can't come up with a good answer except for, "I fucked up."

She studies me closely.

Then sighs.

Fuck, I'm failing her too. I look past her. "I should go help Colt—"

"Oh, no," Colt says. "I've got this." He shifts, starts in on another lug nut. "You just tell your sister how you fucked up things with Joey. She'll help you sort it out."

My eyebrows fly up.

What the fuck?

But he keeps talking before I can process that. "And I'll just lie here...not listening."

I open my mouth to snap at him, but Ky beats me to speaking.

"I was sitting in my car," she says. "Killing time on my phone and then—" Her eyes come to mine and everything inside me stands up straight.

Fuck. "What happened?"

"Well, Colt just pulled up and my video was still playing and I guess it auto-swiped to the next and, well..." For the first time, she looks uncomfortable.

"What, Ky?" I ask. "Tell me."

"It's probably better if I *show* you."

She taps at her phone, then holds it up so I can see the screen.

I jerk when I see Joey's face there, her eyes filled with equal parts devastation and anger. There's a man behind her.

No, not just any man, that asshole kid reporter who kept trying to push her buttons.

"Crap," Kylie says, the phone bobbling as she turns up the volume.

And I hear it:

"A few minutes ago this man, Zach Hiller, recorded me without my knowledge during a painful, heartbreaking conversation..."

Fuck, I never followed up with that little prick.

Never realized who he was.

Hiller's kid? This is—

Hell. I'm in fucking hell.

"As I was trying to go home, planning to cry into a glass of wine while I come to terms with the fact that the man I love may not feel the same way..."

My heart sinks. *"Shit."*

"Yeah, big bro," Kylie murmurs. "You fucked up."

"Yup," Colt agrees.

But I can't acknowledge them.

Because I'm still watching.

And it gets better and worse—the confident way she hands Zach his ass, the agony I see on her face, hear in her voice as she discusses what Travis Hiller did to her, the fear I feel as I watch his son take a threatening step toward her.

But she keeps filming until she's done talking, until the bastard leaves, tires squealing as he tears out of the parking lot.

"I need to go," I whisper. Right fucking now.

Kylie nods. "You really do. But first—" She snags my hand, holding tight, keeping me in place. "Before you go after her, I need you to get your head together. You are not a perfect person—"

A bolt of pain shoots through my chest and I barely hold back my wince.

She sees it anyway.

"Honey," she whispers. "What I *mean* is that you need to cut yourself some slack. You hold yourself to these impossible standards and in doing so, you hurt not just yourself, but also the people you love."

"I know that, Ky."

Except, *do* I?

Because all I can think is that I failed. Again.

"I think what she's saying is that relationships aren't easy." I look up, see that Colt has finished with the tire and is leaning against the trunk, arms and ankles crossed. "Sometimes we hurt the people we love, but what we need to judge ourselves on is what we do to make it right."

I shake my head. "I can't take back the words I spoke to her."

Can't make it all just go away.

"But you can make sure they're replaced with better ones."

I THINK about what Colt said the entire drive to Joey's house.

And I still haven't come up with the right words to replace the bullshit I spouted.

Because I've done anger management, and yeah, I've made a lot of progress, but the rage is still there, and tonight it lashed out and hurt her.

So, how do I protect her from the world if I can't protect her from myself?

"I've tried to be perfect. Killed myself to do everything right —and bad things still happened to me."

So many bad things, and I can never take away that pain from her.

Can never be good enough for her.

Can—

I'm not empty anymore.

I pull into her driveway, her words from weeks before slicing through me.

I did that, *fixed* that.

It's not enough. I need to do more, *be* better—

Killed myself to do everything right—and bad things still happened.

Hell if she's not speaking the truth.

Still, I'm *not* enough. I might never feel like I'm enough, might never feel like I've made this right for her.

And I don't know how to fix—

There's a knock on my window and I jerk, looking up to see Joey standing there. She's beautiful, even with her swollen and red eyes.

Crying. Because of me.

Christ, how can I be this much of a fuck-up?

"Open the door, Damon," she calls.

I realize my engine's still running. I shove the gearshift into park, hit the button to turn off the ignition.

As soon as the locks disengage, she's pulling the door open and a moment after that, another woman I love is tugging me out of my seat.

"Are you okay?" she whispers. "You've been sitting here for ten minutes."

"You've been crying," I whisper back.

Her fingers tighten around my arm, and then she nods. "Yeah."

More pain. More shame.

"That asshole kid is Hiller's son. I-I didn't know. I didn't check—"

She presses her fingers to my lips, then drops her hand to her side, wraps it around mine and draws me toward the house. The front door is open, and she closes it before I can. The lock *clicks* as she engages it, and then she turns away, starts for the kitchen.

I follow her on wooden legs.

She pulls out a stool, orders, "Sit."

Then goes to the fridge and pulls out two bottles of beer.

"I'm supposed to be the one who fixes things," I say... because I don't have anything else.

Her movements don't falter—she uses a bottle opener to pop off the caps, sets a beer in front of me, then sits on the stool next to mine, and announces, "That doesn't work for me."

I jerk so hard I nearly topple off my seat. "You love me."

Her head swivels, eyes coming to mine, brows lifting in question.

"I saw the video."

"Then you know that's true," she says and the barest hint of humor crawls into those gorgeous green eyes. "I should probably be reeling, unraveling, panicking that however many people saw that shit...but, truth is, I finally feel like I can breathe again."

"That's good, baby," I murmur. "And I need you to know I love you too."

She's quiet for a blip. "I know," she eventually says. "I realized that about ten minutes into my crying jag, when my knee was yelling at me for doing it on the kitchen floor. But..." Sad green eyes. "This isn't working for me."

Goddamn that hurts.

"It's not because I don't love you," she says, the words coming fast and furious. "It's not because being in a relationship with you is bad. It's the opposite. The last couple of months have been...*perfect*." Her mouth kicks up on one side. "But this was bound to happen at some point, we both know it."

"I'll go through the anger management program again," I say in a rush, skipping acceptance and going right to panic and bargaining. "I'll get it under control, I promise. I know I can't take back the words I said, but I won't—"

"Damon—"

"I won't ever go there again. I swear, baby. I—"

"Sweetheart."

God, that hurts so fucking much. I'm losing her and she's calling me *sweetheart*.

"I'm sorry," I say.

"I know," she whispers.

"I love you."

"I know that too," she says gently. "And that's why we're here, having this conversation instead of me ignoring your car in the driveway." She sets her beer down, leans toward me, her hand resting on my forearm. "I love you, but I can't be in a relationship with someone who doesn't talk to me, who doesn't share their worries and concerns with me."

"I—"

"So, I'm going to need you to work on that."

I blink. "What?"

"We're going to make a commitment to talk to each other and communicate and not hide important shit." Her hand tightens. "And if we can't figure out a way to do that on our own, we'll find a therapist to help us. Because, Damon, it was never about a sentence or one slip of your temper." She cups my jaw. "You're not perfect, sweetheart."

"Why does everyone keep saying that?" I mutter.

"Who?" she asks quietly.

"Kylie."

Her face softens. "Of course." A blip before her expression turns deadly serious. "I don't expect you to be perfect. Both of us have spent far too much time on that particular occupation. I want us to have joy and love, passion and imperfection. I want you, just you, because I know that I'm everything you want too."

"Red—"

Fingers on my lips for a brief moment, staying my words. "Before you start arguing and self-flagellating, do you remember what I promised you?"

I frown. "No."

"Weeks ago," she says, sliding her hand from my jaw down to my chest. "After coos, after realizing that I felt more alive, more *full* than I've ever felt before...I told you I was going to return the favor."

My heart spasms. "Baby."

"Do you feel empty, sweetheart?"

"*Baby.*"

Her mouth curves. "So we'll work on filling you up."

"Christ, you're incredible," I murmur, covering her hand with mine. Then I can't resist it any longer, I draw her into my arms, hold her as tightly as I dare. "The entire drive over here I've been trying to think of what I can say to make it better, to take away the hurt my words invoked, and then you go and say all of that, say everything that you said in your video." I pull back, cup both of her cheeks, holding her stare so she knows how serious I am. "I am in awe of you, Red."

Her throat works, those eyes glazing over with tears. "The feeling's mutual, hot shot."

And...I find that I have the words.

"No more me hiding shit," I promise. "I'll discuss things with you like a responsible adult."

She smiles.

"And I promise that if I can't fix this shit in my head, the shit that had me shut down and then lash out, I'll find someone who'll help me with it."

"Thank you," she whispers.

"No, baby, thank *you*." I settle my forehead against hers. "For being smart and wonderful and patient and kind and for —" My throat gets tight, the words stoppering up.

"For kicking your future self in the ass, as needed?"

I chuckle. And the words come easier. "No," I say. "Thank you for being you. And thank you for letting me love you, exactly as you are."

"No more secrets," she whispers.

"No more secrets," I vow.

"And lots and lots of sundaes."

I touch her cheek. "And syrup."

"And coos."

Laughter bubbles up in my chest, and I know, finally know, that while things won't always go perfectly and I will definitely fuck up again and we have a huge legal mess to deal with in the morning, that right now I've made it better.

No, that was Joey.

Because for the first time ever...

It doesn't matter that the person making it right wasn't me.

EPILOGUE

Joey, Six Months Later

THE WHISTLE GOES...

And pandemonium explodes—the crowd roars, the guys' equipment hits the ice in a chaotic jumble of sticks and gloves and helmets. There are hugs all around, smacks on the back, huge smiles that threaten to split our faces.

Because we've won.

Because we fucking *did* it.

The Cup is ours.

After eighty-two games. After four brutal rounds of the playoffs that were filled with fights and injuries and two bouts of triple overtime, we've *done* it.

Kaitlyn grins at me. Tommy claps me on the back. Dave is his normal quiet, but I don't miss that his eyes are misty. He'll probably only be coaching for another season or two, so winning this now, *here*, after all the adversity we've faced...

It means a lot.

It means *everything*.

My gaze drifts away from my coaches, slides through the stands, not stopping until it reaches a box poised high above the red line.

Okay, so it doesn't mean *everything*.

Because my life isn't just the job, isn't just hockey anymore.

I have a summer RV trip planned with Beth and John. We're going to hit up Yellowstone—though, Damon and I have our own camper because I'm not sleeping on a table that folds into a bed, not even for Beth and John.

Who am I kidding?

If they asked, I would have bent over backward to accommodate that request.

But Beth had emailed the reservation confirmation, told me she picked out a great RV for us that will "allow Damon and you the privacy young lovers need."

Needless to say, she's beyond the moon that we've navigated our way to happiness.

And currently up in the owner's box, likely chattering Damon's ear off, John next to her, looking on with quiet pride.

Or maybe John has called it and ended up in the stands because listening to Kylie and Beth's nervous babbling as the game wound down got to be too much for him.

Speaking of Kylie, our Girls' Nights are regular, our crocheting didn't get any better, and my spidey sense of something happening between her and Colt has been pinging off the charts lately.

There's something there, even if she denies it.

Maybe even because she denies it *too* much.

Either way, I have my eye on that, and it's one of the few things I haven't shared with Damon. Yes, it's technically breaking my promise to be open and truthful about all things, but as the counselor we've been seeing once a week has stated on more than one occasion, there are a few truths we can keep to ourselves."

Like, *Yes, Beth, your meatloaf is delicious.*

And, *Of course, those jeans are flattering, Ky.*

And, *No, sweetheart, your sister isn't a sexual being. Nope. Absolutely not.*

The rest of it, though, Damon and I have both put the work in, and we're good.

We're *great*.

Even the scandal that followed my social media showdown with Zach Hiller worked out far better than I could have ever hoped for—with my and the others' permission, the D.A. moved quickly, offering Travis a plea deal that saw him seeing jail time. Not nearly enough, it won't *ever* be enough.

But it was something.

And those few months in jail were nothing when compared to the public backlash he faced, especially as more women came out with their own accusations.

But I'm moving forward, putting it all to bed.

Of course, I spent the month after the infamous video doing far more interviews than I ever wanted, talking about what happened too damned much...all while trying to coach. But the funny thing was, the more I talked about it, the more I heard about other people's experiences—*people* because it wasn't just women who shared with me—the more that seed of strength inside me grew.

Like the first slender stalk had popped out of the soil that night I confronted Zach, but it was just a beginning.

And now it's grown into something beautiful.

Even though it began in pain.

Kind of like this moment—lost sleep and injuries and fail-ures, years of struggling, battling, *surviving*, grinding out games and crying when trades meant losing someone I cared about, the stress, the pressure...all of it has coalesced into...

This.

Watching my guys each take their turn to hoist the Cup.

It's beauty and joy and having the insane urge to start all over again so we can get right back here.

Grinning, I start to turn for the hall, ready to leave them to their celebration—or maybe to go find my man so we can do some celebrating of our own, but I barely make it a quarter-rotation before ringing echoes through the arena—and not that of the crowd.

I freeze, head cocking, listening hard.

Because that legit sounds like a cell phone ringing.

I spin back to the ice and...all of a sudden, there's a mic in my face. "Um..."

The operator just grins, and I understand why a moment later because a voice comes on that I know better than my own.

"Hey, Red." My eyes shoot to the Jumbotron, heart squeezing when I see Damon, standing there looking like a god in his gorgeous suit, his face soft, his eyes burning just for me.

The microphone wiggles, prompting me to reply, "Hey, sweetheart."

The crowd quiets just in time for him to say, "I have a question to ask you."

Now my heart is rolling over in my chest, my pulse thundering to my veins. I don't care that the guys are watching me, that twenty-thousand-plus gazes are likely glued to me. I just ask, "What's that?"

His grin widens. "Well, you know I love you, and you love me—"

There's a collective inhalation from all around me.

"And you're the absolute best thing that has ever happened to me..."

Someone says, "Aw!" and my lips curve up.

"I feel the same about you," I say into the microphone.

More of the crowd joins in with an "Aw," and I don't miss that I'm suddenly surrounded by smirking hockey players.

Christ, I'm never going to live this down.

And I don't fucking care.

"So...I wanted to ask if you'd do me the honor of marrying me."

There's another inhalation...or maybe that's just me, because I can barely hear myself over my pounding heart, can barely force my lungs to keep drawing in air and letting it out again.

He asked—

Holy shit.

Then the crowd starts chanting, "Say yes! Say yes! Say yes!" and every cell in my body screams at me to just blurt out my "Yes!" and turn into a blubbering mess.

But then...the mischief takes over.

I look up at the box high overhead, grin, and say, "I'll have you know I don't talk about my personal life in public."

The crowd roars, laughter and cheers mingling at the blatant lie.

"Well, I guess that means I'd better get down here and ask you myself."

I still.

Because that last sentence didn't boom its way through the arena's speakers.

It's said from a couple of feet behind me.

Slowly, I turn around...and see that Damon's on one knee just behind the bench.

"Come here, Red," he orders.

"But you hate phone calls," I blurt inanely.

"And yet"—his smile is the most beautiful thing I've ever seen—"I just made the most important one of my life."

I throw myself into his arms, and—spoiler alert—I turn into that blubbering mess. He doesn't falter, just catches me close, holding me tightly against him, my tears soaking into his suit. His head drops, lips coming to my ear.

"Does this mean you say yes?"

Colt, Four Months Later

I crouch and unscrew the little black cap, press the tip of the ballpoint pen against the valve.

Air hisses out in a rush.

The tire slowly goes flat.

Is this a crime? Probably.

Is this the first time I've done this? Nope.

Kylie Connors is probably wondering why in the fuck she gets so many flat tires. And I'm the answer. Because every time she ends up with a flat—and this will be the fifth—I'm there to fix it for her.

Because it's the only time she'll acknowledge my presence.

Not when she tags along to the team events. Not when we come across each other in the halls of the practice rink or the Sierra's home arena. Not after games or before practice or if we happen to run into each other in town.

It's only when she's trapped on the side of the dark, quiet road that she'll talk to me.

Look at me.

And what she gives me during those short moments...it's fucking beautiful. She's funny and smart and—

Intoxicating.

Irresistible.

Still, I've tried. To give her space, to let her come to me if and when she decides. To not push even though every part of me demands it.

I know what she went through, know it still haunts her.

So, I waited.

I just...can't any longer.

I pull the tip of the pen out, survey my handiwork—low enough she shouldn't immediately notice, but enough air gone that she won't make it far.

Perfect. I screw on the cap, slink away to my car, and climb in.

Then I sit and wait for her to walk out of the arena.

To climb into her own car, start up the engine.

And when she drives out of the lot...

I follow.

Because I'm done waiting for Kylie Connors to come to me.

Tonight, everything changes.

I hope you enjoyed Joey and Damon's story of perseverance, finding the strength to allow love in, and all those phone calls! :)

Don't miss the final book in the Sierra Hockey series, ATTACKING THE ZONE. **I'm done waiting for her to come to me. Tonight...everything changes.**

CLICK HERE TO READ ATTACKING THE
ZONE NOW>

And do you want a sneak peek into my BRAND NEW hockey series?

If you love big, bearded hockey players who fall hard and fast for the women they love, pick up book one in the Grizzlies Hockey series, MARRIED TO NUMBER TWENTY-TWO NOW>. **I signed the contract. I just didn't expect her to show up ten years later, ready to cash it in.**

CLICK HERE TO READ MARRIED TO NUMBER TWENTY-TWO NOW>

READ on for a sneak peek below!

Aiden

I wake up to a heavy knock on my condo's front door and glare blearily at my phone in the charger.

"Two in the fucking morning," I mutter, grabbing a pillow and clamping it over my ears. "It's two o'clock in the morning on my fucking birthday, and I have to deal with this shit."

This shit being my neighbors.

It's not the first time they've pounded drunk on my door, desperate for their roommate to let them in to what they think is their apartment.

This was sort of funny the first time.

I remember those days, drinking too much, being dumb.

But after the second and the third—where I gained status into the inner circle and a code to the keypad to their apartment door—it was no longer cute.

Now, six months later and countless times of bailing them out, I'm *so* not in the mood.

Especially when it's my fucking birthday.

The knocking cuts off and I think—*pray*—that they've gotten the hint.

But it's approximately two seconds later when it starts up again.

I glance at my phone again, see that really five minutes have passed, making it two-seventeen and officially my birthday.

Some present.

I could try to ignore it—but that just means extending the torture. Sighing, I toss back the blankets and stomp to my apartment door, whipping it open to reveal a slender brunette on my doorstep.

"Ho, mama," she says, gaze taking a slow perusal down my body.

"Who the fuck are you?"

"It's me. Luna."

I stare at her, uncomprehendingly.

"From Rockfield?" she adds.

Recognition begins to dawn. "Luna Maybelle?"

"Yup! That's me." She nods, grinning, and I see it then, the glimpse of my best friend from the childhood rink I grew up playing at come out in her smile. Mischief and life. Joy and hard work.

Summers spent spending every spare moment together— her figure skating, me playing hockey.

But she's not little Luna anymore.

Christ, she's anything but—tall, beautiful, curves for days— and she's staring at me.

Because I'm staring at her.

Fucking hell.

I spur myself into motion.

"Luna! Oh my God!" I pull her into a hug. "What the hell are you doing here?"

"It's your birthday!" She holds up a piece of paper that looks faintly familiar. "And, well, it's mine too, remember?"

That's right.

We have the same birthday.

"We're both twenty-five, single, and—"

My eyes narrow in on the paper. It's crumpled and stained, as though it's years old.

A purple and pink swirl decorates the edges and suddenly I remember her painstakingly drawing it as we sat side-by-side at one of the high top tables of the ice rink, waiting for the Zamboni to finish cutting the ice.

Her brow had been furrowed. Her movements carefully controlled.

And I had been obsessing over how pink her lips were and what her butt looked like in her skating dress, so much so that I barely remember what we'd been drawing.

No, I think hard, grabbing on to those memories, not what we'd been *drawing*.

The contract we'd put together.

The contract my hormonal twelve-year-old self had signed.

With a sparkly pink colored pencil.

A giant boulder settles in my stomach, but before I can snap myself out of the horror of those memories, she shoves the paper in my hands then throws her arms around my neck.

"We're getting married!"

CLICK HERE TO READ MARRIED TO NUMBER TWENTY-TWO NOW>

Hate missing Elise's new releases? Love contests, exclusive excerpts and giveaways?
Then signup for Elise's newsletter here!

www.elisefaber.com/newsletter

And join Elise's fan group, the Fabinators (https://www.facebook.com/groups/fabinators) for insider information, sneak peaks at new releases, and fun freebies! Hope to see you there!

If you enjoy my series, considering supporting me on PATREON! Get access to early releases, bonus content, character art, audiobooks, special edition covers, swag, and much more!

CLICK HERE TO SUPPORT ME>

I so appreciate your help in spreading the word about my books, including sharing with friends! Please leave a review on your favorite book site!

SIERRA HOCKEY

ALSO BY ELISE FABER

Broken

Boldly

Breathless

Ballsy

Bewitched

Blowout

Breathe

Blazed

Sierra Hockey Series

Over the Line

Caught from Behind

The Big Skate

On the Fly

Attacking the Zone

Eagles Hockey Series (all stand alone)

Broken Laces

Lace 'em Up

Knotted Laces

Loaded Laces

Lucky Laces

Oak Ridge Vineyards

Bottles & Blades

Beauty & the Boardroom

Rush Hockey Trilogy #1

Big Puck Energy

Filthy Puckboy

So Pucking Over It

Rush Hockey Trilogy #2

Love, Pucks, and Other Stories

All's Fair in Pucks and War

No Pucks Lost Between Us

Rush Hockey Novellas

Puck and Make Up

Billionaire's Club (**all stand alone**)

Bad Night Stand

Bad Breakup

Bad Husband

Bad Hookup

Bad Divorce

Bad Fiancé

Bad Boyfriend

Bad Blind Date

Bad Wedding

Bad Engagement

Bad Bridesmaid

Bad Swipe

Bad Girlfriend

Bad Best Friend

Bad Rebound

Bad Romance

Bad Business

Bad Billionaire's Quickies

Love, Action, Camera (all stand alone)

Dotted Line

Action Shot

Close-Up

End Scene

Meet Cute

Love After Midnight **(all stand alone)**

Rum And Notes

Virgin Daiquiri

On The Rocks

Sex On The Seats

Life Sucks Series

Train Wreck

Hot Mess

Dumpster Fire

Clusterf*@k

FUBAR

Perfect Storm

Free Fall

Lost Cause

Roosevelt Ranch Series **(all stand alone, series complete)**

Disaster at Roosevelt Ranch

Heartbreak at Roosevelt Ranch

Collision at Roosevelt Ranch

Regret at Roosevelt Ranch

Desire at Roosevelt Ranch

Phoenix Series **(read in order)**

Phoenix Rising

Dark Phoenix

Phoenix Freed

Phoenix: LexTal Chronicles **(rereleasing soon, stand alone, Phoenix world)**

From Ashes

In Flames

To Smoke

KTS Series (all stand alone, series complete)

Riding The Edge

Crossing The Line

Leveling The Field

Scorching The Earth

Cocky Heroes World

Tattooed Troublemaker

ABOUT THE AUTHOR

USA Today bestselling author, Elise Faber, loves chocolate, Star Wars, Harry Potter, and hockey (the order depending on the day and how well her team -- the Sharks! -- are playing). She and her husband also play as much hockey as they can squeeze into their schedules, so much so that their typical date night is spent on the ice. Elise is the mom to two exuberant boys and lives in Northern California. Connect with her in her Facebook group, the Fabinators or find more information about her books at www.elisefaber.com.

f facebook.com/elisefaberauthor

a amazon.com/author/elisefaber

BB bookbub.com/profile/elise-faber

O instagram.com/elisefaber

d tiktok.com/@elisefaberauthor

g goodreads.com/elisefaber

www.ingramcontent.com/pod-product-compliance
Lightning Source LLC
Chambersburg PA
CBHW070635100726
47907CB00007B/1993